THE EHRICH WEISZ

CHRONICLES

METAMORPHOSIS

THE EHRICH WEISZ

CHRONICLES

METAMORPHOSIS

MARTY CHAN

Fitzhenry & Whiteside

Published in Canada by Fitzhenry & Whiteside
195 Allstate Parkway, Markham, ON   L3R 4T8

Published in the United States by Fitzhenry & Whiteside
311 Washington Street, Brighton, MA   02135

2 4 6 8 10 9 7 5 3 1

Library and Archives Canada Cataloguing in Publication
Title: Metamorphosis / Marty Chan
Names: Chan, Marty, author.
Series: Chan, Marty. Ehrich Weisz chronicles.
Description: Series statement: The Ehrich Weisz chronicles
Identifiers: Canadiana 20190114703 | ISBN 9781554553921 (softcover)
Classification: LCC PS8555.H39244 M48 2019 | DDC jC813/.6—dc23

Library and Archives Canada Cataloguing in Publication
Title: Metamorphosis / Marty Chan
Names: Chan, Marty, author.
Series: Chan, Marty. Ehrich Weisz chronicles.
Description: Series statement: The Ehrich Weisz chronicles
Identifiers: Canadiana 20190114703 | ISBN 9781554553921 (softcover)
Classification: LCC PS8555.H39244 M48 2019 | DDC jC813/.6—dc23

Fitzhenry & Whiteside acknowledges with thanks the Canada Council for the Arts and the Ontario Arts Council for their support of our publishing program.

We acknowledge the financial support of the Government of Canada through the Canada Book Fund (CBF) for our publishing activities.

 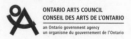

Cover and interior design by Tanya Montini
Printed in Canada by Houghton Boston
www.fitzhenry.ca

ACKNOWLEDGMENTS

A writer never works alone. For all their help along the way, thank you to Penny Hozy, Cheryl Chen, Tanya Montini, Wei Wong, Michelle Chan, Billy Kid, Sheldon Casavant, and Brad Smilanich.

For Dianne Johnstone.
Thank you for your support of the Edmonton Public Library
and your patience with me.

THE VERDICT

New York, June 23 - The *Oriental Clipper* trial concluded yesterday when a jury found 54 people guilty of murder.

The accused stood cheek to jowl on the stage of Madison Square Garden's theatre. The defendants and courtroom spectators awaited the verdict in the makeshift courtroom. When Judge Marcus Thorton read the judgment, the packed theatre of victims' family members erupted in cheers. One grieving mother collapsed in tears. The convicted remained stoic.

The *Oriental Clipper* crashed in the Hudson River on August 13, 1891. Sailors from nearby merchant vessels pulled the survivors from the choppy water, only to discover they were not the airship's passengers or crew but illegal Dimensionals who had skyjacked the craft. The bodies of the crew and passengers—their throats slashed—were found among the wreckage.

Judge Thorton imposed the harshest sentence

allowed under New York law: the death penalty. He concluded the trial with a warning: "This heinous attack is an act of war, and we must send a message that we will not stand idly by while Dimensionals threaten the very safety of our naturalized citizens."

Demon Watch Commissioner Thomas Edison will oversee the execution. The date will be announced shortly.

NO DIMENSIONALS ALLOWED

The sign in the dry goods store window read: "No dogs or dimensionals allowed."

Ehrich Weisz wanted to rip the poster off the glass and shred it. Similar signs had appeared in establishments throughout Manhattan since the *Oriental Clipper* murder trial. Before the incident, New Yorkers tolerated the presence of the travellers who had come from other worlds. Today, they barred Dimensionals from their shops and openly mocked them in the streets. Men spit on green-hued women while mothers yanked their young away from Dimensional children with clawed hands.

Not every Dimensional looked like a monster. Some, like Ehrich, appeared human and could blend in with the populace. He loathed the racist sentiments the frightened and paranoid citizens hollered in the streets. Fear had loosened their tongues and imprisoned their empathy. He wanted to call them fools and cowards, but he did not want to draw any attention to himself. Instead, he gritted his teeth and seethed in silence whenever he heard New Yorkers spew venom about the immigrants.

Right now, he had a mission: find Ole Lukoje, the hook-nosed traveller who had been the bane of Ehrich's existence. Ehrich had first encountered the traveller when he was working for the Demon Watch, and had caught the raggedy man in the act of plucking out a young mother's eyes for his dinner.

Later, Ole Lukoje teamed up with the warlord Ba Tian to help plot the invasion of this world, but Ehrich and his allies were able to thwart the plan. Ba Tian had been trapped in another dimension, but Ole Lukoje had gone into hiding.

The newspaper clipping in Ehrich's hand gave him hope that the raggedy man was still in New York. Ole Lukoje possessed the nano-dust, particles that enabled the man to jump between dimensions. This was the means Ehrich needed to return to his world. He skimmed the paper again, rereading the article about a grisly murder in the neighbourhood. His gaze lingered on one sentence: "The victim had both eyes removed."

Ehrich searched the block near the crime scene, hoping to find some clue that would confirm Ole Lukoje was at large. He needed to find the raggedy man, because he was the only one who could transport Ehrich and his brother Dash home.

Ehrich shifted from one foot to the other, eyeing the crowds in the street. No sign of Ole Lukoje. Ehrich adjusted his fake beard and sidled up to a street vendor hawking oysters. The gap-toothed woman grinned at him and motioned to the half-shells displayed on the top of her wagon.

"Hungry, young man?"

He shook his head. "You work this street a lot?"

Her eyes narrowed. "What's it to you?"

"Thought you might have your ear to the ground about the murder last week."

She shifted back on her heels and sucked in her bottom lip. "You a hunter or someone who likes cheap thrills?"

He reached into his pocket and pulled out some coins. "I'm a fan of your oysters."

She took his money and handed him a plump oyster on a half-shell, then looked both ways before leaning toward Ehrich. "What I've heard is that it was one of them demons that did it."

Ehrich nodded. "I guessed that much. Is the paper correct? Did the killer take her eyes?"

"Heard rumours that she wasn't the first. There have been others, but the police were trying to keep it quiet so as not to panic us. Not much good now. Everyone's on edge."

Ehrich pursed his lips. This had to be the work of Ole Lukoje. He wanted to ask more, but he noticed a pair of Demon Watch hunters strolling toward him.

"Thanks for the oysters," he mumbled and moved on.

"You get hungry again, you be sure to drop by," she called after him.

He waved without looking back and hurried down the street. He stopped in front of a dry goods store and pulled his cap over his eyes. He pretended to peer through the window as he glanced back at the hunters. He had been a fugitive ever since he had abandoned his duties on Demon Watch and sided with Amina and Mr. Serenity, the travellers who fought against the warlord. The hunters continued toward him. Ehrich slipped into the shop.

The proprietor and the old woman at his counter glanced

up. The upright man sported a moustache as stiff as his posture while the woman wore a bustle as wide as the store aisle.

"Afternoon, sir."

"Good day," Ehrich replied.

"Haven't seen you before," the shop owner said, pulling at the suspenders under his apron.

"I moved into the neighbourhood last week," he said. "I came here from the Bowery."

The proprietor raised an eyebrow. "Why were you living there of all places?"

Many Dimensionals had moved into the Bowery's ramshackled tenements—the only places they could afford. Often several families huddled in the same cramped apartments, sharing the same beds, outhouses, and rank air. This was one of the few areas in New York where humans tolerated Dimensionals. To claim residency in the Bowery was to admit you were either a foreigner or sympathetic to the Dimensionals.

Ehrich swept the flat cap off his head to reveal his matted brown hair. "I don't have horns if that's what you're worried about."

The woman snorted. "Filthy creatures. All of them."

"What do you need?" the proprietor asked.

Ehrich glanced out the window. The hunters strolled past, not even glancing inside. He relaxed his stance and smiled. "Spoons and forks. I'm tired of eating with my hands."

"Two aisles down."

Ehrich waved thanks. He pretended to scan the goods on the shelves, eyeing the window to make sure the pair hadn't backtracked. His gaze lingered at a section of kids toys. A box of clay marbles stared back at him. He picked up three of them and cradled them in his palm. They reminded him of the marbles his kid brother Dash owned before they crossed over to this dimension. Ehrich rolled the clay balls around, letting them clack together, remembering how skilled Dash was at knocking other kids' marbles out of the circle.

He was about to put the marbles back when he heard a snort. A young boy with a runny nose stared at a glass jar of sweets. He reminded Ehrich of Dash. His hands in his pockets, the boy never took his eyes off of the hard candy. Ehrich walked over and plucked the lid off. He reached inside, pulled out a red stick, and placed the hard candy in his hand. The boy raised his eyebrows and leaned in as Ehrich closed his fist and blew on it. He opened his hand—empty. The boy's eyes widened and his mouth dropped.

"How did you do that?"

Ehrich plucked the red stick from behind the boy's ear. "You must be made of this stuff."

The boy beamed. Ehrich missed performing for an audience. He offered the sweet and the boy pulled his hands out of his pockets. Each hand had seven fingers. The boy spotted Ehrich staring, grabbed the candy, and jammed his hands back into hiding.

"Hey!" the proprietor yelled. "What are you doing?"

"Nothing!" the young boy squealed, his eyes burning with shame.

"Pull your hands out of your pocket."

"Why?"

"Pull them out."

Ehrich tried to explain. "I was showing him a magic trick."

The boy slowly pulled his hands out of his pocket with the red candy in one deformed hand.

"Oh, mercy! He's one of them," gasped the old woman.

The shop owner stormed over, grabbed the boy by the wrist, and hauled him to the counter. The boy struggled and kicked, but the angry owner refused to release him. Other customers gathered to witness the confrontation.

Ehrich drew closer to the boy.

"He's not even human," the shop owner said. "Look at his deformed hand. Can't have their kind here."

"Will I catch a disease from that thing?" the old woman asked. "I brushed against it."

The boy stammered, "Um, ah, I didn't mean to put this in my pocket. It's just that—"

"Save your lies for Demon Watch, you little monster. Someone get the authorities."

"I saw a pair down the street," a beefy man bellowed. He headed toward the door.

Ehrich stiffened. He couldn't be caught in the store. "Be careful of the kid's hand," he warned.

The man hesitated. "Why?"

"Didn't you read the paper about the murder? What if that kid is the killer? That hand is probably a powerful weapon. Might be poisoned stingers in the fingertips. Show him your hands, kid."

The boy raised his hands and showed the back of them to the shop owner. The fingernails on the two extra fingers blinked at the beefy man, who now retreated. The extra appendages were stems with eyes.

Ehrich yelled at the boy. "Run!"

The beefy man blocked the door. Ehrich grabbed the boy by the collar, hauling him out of the man's reach. He veered to the left as he snatched an iron skillet from a shelf and hurled it at the shop window. The glass shattered and cascaded to the ground. Brisk air blew into the store.

Ehrich hoisted the boy by the armpits and launched him through the opening. He followed. Glass crunched under his boots and he nearly slipped on the shards when he landed on the cobblestone street. Bystanders gaped at the scene.

"Demons!" Ehrich shouted as he pointed back into the store. "They tried to kill our brother. Run!"

The stunned bystanders didn't react at first. The man appeared at the broken window. Ehrich yelled. "That's one of them!"

This spurred the bystanders to action. They rushed to grab the man climbing out of the shop. A melee erupted. Fists flew along with a few loose teeth.

Ehrich glanced down the street at the hunters, who were now rushing to the shop, and bolted away with the boy in tow. He ran past the row of dry goods stores and restaurants through a phalanx of peddlers selling vegetables. When the crowd thinned, Ehrich slowed and released the boy's arm.

"You okay, kid?"

The boy smiled. "Why did you help me?"

"I know I don't look it, but we're the same. You know what I'm talking about?"

"Yes." The boy rubbed his reddened wrist. "Well, thanks."

"What's your name?"

"Gur-Rahim," the boy answered.

"I'm Ehrich. You've got to be careful about those hands. Stick around the Bowery and blend in."

"I can't. We need food."

"What about your parents?"

"My mother can't find a new job. Not since they shut down the Hudson River tunnel project."

"Well, your best bet is to hang around the street vendors at the end of the day. You can get their food for cheap or free if you know how to ask."

Gur-Rahim cocked his head to one side. "How do you know?"

"I've spent some time out here."

The boy scurried away, hustling past a corn vendor who barked about her fresh hot corn. Other peddlers hawked their wares from wooden pushcarts to busy New Yorkers haggling for a bargain. The briny odour of raw oysters mingled with the smell of bodies. Ehrich glanced back. No sign of pursuers. But after talking to the oyster vendor, he was sure Ole Lukoje was still in New York.

•—WW—•

The travellers from other dimensions huddled in ragtag groups along the Hudson River. Yellow-faced women leaned against the walls of warehouses, trying to catch a few winks of sleep. Cyclops men paced the street. A group of squid-like travellers played cards on top of a table made of crates. They glared at the fence separating them from the Hudson River tunnel project and the human guards that patrolled the barrier.

Amina paced along the length of the fence. As she surveyed the travellers, she couldn't help but think of the refugee camps she'd spent time in after the warlord Ba Tian had destroyed her world. The raven-skinned girl had fled the ruins of her home and lived hand to mouth along with survivors in makeshift settlements. The grind of the hopeless routine had worn her down until she and her fellow refugees stared glassy-eyed at one another. They no longer saw the world in front of them—only the fog of a bleak future and wisps of their past lives. She recognized the same futile looks in the travellers camped along the street.

Before the New Yorkers turned on them, the travellers earned their keep by digging a tunnel under the Hudson River to connect a subway train to Manhattan. The company had suspended the work after the attack on the *Oriental Clipper*. With no other promises of employment, all the workers could do was wait for the tunnel project to re-open.

What they did not know was that under the tunnel was a secret base that Ba Tian's operatives had built in preparation for the invasion. Buried deep under the rock was an arsenal of exoskeleton war machines that could wipe out the entire city. She knew Ba Tian had been trapped in another dimension and his generals had been thrown into prison after the *Oriental Clipper* attack, but she feared that one of the generals might have slipped away. For all she knew, that general was now under the tunnel with a faction of Ba Tian's army, preparing the exoskeletons for an invasion.

She knew the war wasn't over and she had the scars across her body to remind her what would happen if Ba Tian's soldiers regained control of the exoskeletons. She wanted to make certain no enemies would ever use the machines under her feet, and the only way to do that was to secure the exoskeletons first.

Amina slowed when she reached a warehouse at the far end of the encampment. Fewer travellers gathered here because of the open exposure to the wind blowing off of the Hudson River. She nodded to her companion, a lanky man with a moustache and a copy of the *New York World*. Nikola Tesla folded the newspaper, tucked it under his arm, and smiled at her.

"Anything new?"

She shook her head. "No sign of activity. At least as far as I can tell from out here. If we could get behind the fence ..."

"Not even worth considering. The last thing we want is to draw attention to ourselves. A battle with the guards would do just that."

"I know, but I could slip past them when night falls. I'm sure I could find a weak spot in their security."

"You've probed the fence at least ten times already." She shrugged. "There has to be another way in."

"Amina, if we can't get past those guards, I'm positive Ba Tian's soldiers won't be able to. The guards are both a blessing and a curse."

"We have to get below before the enemy does."

"We can't do this alone. How do you expect us to storm the fence?"

"Not an attack, Mr. Tesla. One or two of us might be able to slip past the guards."

"And what if you get captured?"

"Better than to sit here and wait!"

Silence.

"I'm sorry I snapped, sir."

He nodded. "I understand your frustration, Amina, but we need more bodies before we do anything. Perhaps some of the soldiers in Purgatory."

She shook her head. "We need them to continue training the civilians. Prepare them for battle."

"Is all this preparation necessary? Ba Tian is trapped in another dimension. His generals and soldiers are in prison. What more do we have to fear?"

"We cannot be sure that all of his generals were captured and the rest of his army is spread across other dimensions. Who knows how many have made their way here? If we had the exoskeletons, we would even the odds."

"Or you could get captured and we'd have to find a way to rescue you."

She eyed the guards along the fence. "I won't get caught."

"Caught doing what?" Ehrich asked as he jogged toward the pair.

"You're late," Amina said.

"I think I have a lead on Ole Lukoje. There was a murder last week. The victim's eyes were taken."

"Intriguing," Tesla said, plucking the newspaper from under his arm. "I was just reading about a break-in at Thomas Edison's Orange County facility. Apparently, a guard was killed. His eyes were taken."

Ehrich stiffened. "Ole Lukoje."

"We don't know that for sure," Amina said.

Tesla cocked his head to one side. "It would appear to be more than a coincidence. Once the man has retrieved his nano-dust, who knows what he will do. Perhaps, he could summon all of Ba Tian's army."

Amina shook her head. "No, I think he can only transport one or two people at a time. Otherwise, all of Ba Tian's forces would be swarming the city by now. Still, he might be bringing over a few of Ba Tian's soldiers as we speak."

"The only way to know for sure is to look for Ole Lukoje," Ehrich said. "He's my way home."

Amina shook her head. "We have to get to those exoskeletons before Ba Tian's people do."

"We don't know if there are any generals left, Amina, and as long as guards are posted here, I doubt they are going to let any Dimensionals through," Tesla said.

"We can't take the chance," Amina argued. "We have to get below."

"We don't have enough people to do that," he said. "We barely found enough to keep watch on the tunnel project."

"The soldiers have their hands full with training right now. We have to prepare for war."

"A war that might never happen. Amina, let's put this to rest for now. At the very least, let's bring Mr. Serenity up to speed and feed ourselves. I'm famished."

Before she could argue, Tesla set off down the road. Ehrich cast a sideways glance at Amina and shrugged. "You coming?"

She sighed, taking one last look at the guards on the fence before joining the pair.

THE WAY HOME

Deep under Manhattan, Purgatory teemed with inter-dimensional travellers. Trying to piece their lives together after fleeing their war-torn worlds, some of the travellers sold wares and made the best of their lives under the network of pneumatic tubes that crisscrossed over the steel and glass structures of the underground city. The soldiers trained the most able-bodied civilians to fight.

Ehrich, Tesla, and Amina walked along a training area where a battle-worn soldier barked orders at civilians.

"Hands up! Block first, strike second! Keep your feet planted! Attack! Lunge! Don't hesitate!"

Some of the civilians learned faster than others. One was on the ground gasping for air. The blue-faced instructor with a Cyclops eye gave her no pause.

"On your feet! Ba Tian's soldiers aren't going to wait for you to catch your breath."

She slowly rose to her feet and resumed the training. Amina nodded at the Cyclops soldier. He grunted at her and continued with the training.

The trio headed toward the market square, their boots clicking against the smooth obsidian surface as they passed food stalls. Not every civilian trained for war. These vendors were deemed unfit for combat either because of physical or emotional trauma. The aroma of exotic fruit and vegetables teased Ehrich's nose. He inhaled deeply and his appetite grew. He quickened the pace, veering to a vendor with skewers of barbecued meat on his cart. He sat in a wheel chair. He had no legs.

"How much for the meat?" Tesla inquired.

The purple-skinned vendor held up five fingers.

"You're ripping me off, my friend," he said.

"We'll give you two," Ehrich offered.

He shook his head.

Amina pleaded, "Can we skip the haggling?"

"That's part of the fun." Ehrich turned to the vendor. "Two and that's my final offer."

"You do what you want," Amina said. "I'm going to track down recruits for the watch." She walked off.

"Don't you want something to eat first?" But it was too late. Amina was already out of earshot.

The vendor held up five fingers.

Tesla chuckled. "You could buy one less skewer, Ehrich. It wouldn't hurt for you to lose a pound or two."

Ehrich scowled. "Fine. Five. Hold on. Let me check what I have." He fished three marbles out of his trouser pockets.

The vendor clucked, "I prefer real money."

Ehrich ignored him as he rolled the balls on the palm of his hand. In the chaos at the dry goods store, he had shoved them in his pocket. They were similar to the ones Dash had lost to the bully in Ehrich's home world.

—✷—

Ehrich's hands fumbled as he tried to pick the lock to the apartment door. Behind him, Dash nervously kept watch.

"Gregor can keep my marbles," Dash said, shifting from one foot to another."

"No, he stole them from you. We're getting them back."

Suddenly, the door swung open and a red-faced man roared at the brothers. Ehrich froze with his lockpick set in his hands.

"Thieves!"

"Run," Ehrich yelled as he slipped away from Gregor's father.

He hurtled down the steps of the apartment building and shoved his brother out of the doorway. The thundering steps of Gregor's father echoed in Ehrich's ears.

He pushed Dash to the left and barked, "Split up! He can't catch both of us."

The brothers parted. Ehrich drew Gregor's father after him. The chase led them through the streets of Appleton, their home town. Ehrich kept ahead of the man, running past curious onlookers until he was sure that Dash was away safely. Then he gave the man the slip and searched for his brother.

But it seemed Dash had disappeared. Ehrich searched up and down the streets, careful not to stumble across Gregor's father again. Finally, Ehrich spotted Dash at the outskirts of the neighbourhood, but his brother seemed different.

"Dash? What's wrong?" Ehrich asked.

The young boy ignored him and stiffly marched toward the

town cemetery, clutching a medallion around his neck. Ehrich
had never seen this thing before. He followed, trying to get a
sense of what Dash was up to.

He never anticipated what he witnessed next. His brother stood
in the middle of grave markers and a rift in the air appeared,
revealing a myriad of other worlds. He was about to step through.

"No!" Ehrich screamed as he rushed to stop Dash.

The younger Weisz struggled to get away from Ehrich. In the fight,
the two brothers fell into the rift, falling for what seemed like forever.
Then hard ground met with Ehrich's shoulder and he lost his grip
on his brother. When Ehrich regained his senses, he found himself in
New York City. His brother ran away and disappeared in the
crowd. Ehrich started after him but a carriage nearly ran him over.

When Ehrich made his way to the other side of the busy street,
Dash was nowhere in sight. He was gone. The only thing Ehrich
had of his brother was the strange medallion he had ripped
from Dash's neck during the fight: the Infinity Coil.

—◦∿∿◦—

"If you're not hungry, Ehrich, I'll gladly eat yours," Tesla said.

Ehrich rolled the marbles in his hand one last time before
pocketing them. "Thanks," he said, taking the skewer from the
vendor. The smell of cumin and lamb wafted up his nostrils.

Tesla cocked his head to the side. "What are the marbles for?"

"Dash used to have some like these back in the other ... in my
world," he replied.

"He's a little old to play with marbles, wouldn't you agree?"

"They might trigger old memories. Help him connect to the
past, before Kifo."

"You might have a stronger impact than them," Tesla said

Ehrich said nothing. He felt too guilty to spend any real time with Dash. He blamed himself for everything that had happened after they had arrived in this dimension. Ehrich couldn't find his brother for several years. His only lead came when he found Amina and Mr. Serenity, who revealed the true power of the Infinity Coil. His brother's soul was trapped within the medallion while an assassin, Kifo, possessed the boy's body. The assassin worked for the warlord, Ba Tian, who destroyed worlds to plunder them of their riches.

Ehrich had ultimately succeeded in freeing Dash from the Infinity Coil and Kifo, but the price had been dear. They had lost an important ally, Ba Tian's daughter—Ning Shu. She had turned against her father and would have been instrumental in bringing an end to the invasion. She had died during the fight against Kifo. Dash was free, but Ning Shu was gone forever.

Now that Dash was back, however, he seemed different. Perhaps it was the time he had been trapped in the Infinity Coil or maybe Dash blamed Ehrich for all that had happened, but Dash did not seem like the boy Ehrich remembered.

"He's your brother," Tesla continued, "and every moment you spend with him will help him remember who he once was. With or without the marbles."

Ehrich closed his fist around the orbs and said nothing.

"When I was a boy, almost the same age as your brother, the army tried to recruit me. I was a frail teenager, and my parents knew this was a death sentence for me. They sent me away to live in the mountains. I survived through the bitter winter, hunting for my own food and finding shelter where I could. It was not easy, but despite all expectations I survived. Do you know what got me through the harshest nights?"

Ehrich shook his head.

"The thought of my family."

"What if I'm not enough?"

"You will be, Ehrich. You will be."

They walked away from the marketplace, eating in silence.

•—WWW—•

In the glass tower at the outer edge of Purgatory, Dash perched on his bed in the quarters he shared with his brother. He stared at the wall, or more accurately, he seemed to be staring through it as if he were trying to will himself to go somewhere else.

Ehrich entered the room, holding out the clay marbles. "Dash, look what I found."

The younger Weisz glanced at the balls then turned his attention back to the wall.

"They're like the ones you used to play with," Ehrich said. "You used to be so good at marbles. Want to play now?"

Silence.

"Here, let's set up a circle right between our beds." Ehrich grabbed a chalk from the nightstand beside his bed and drew a circle on the tiled floor. He placed a marble in the centre then handed one to Dash.

"Knock the marble out of the circle. You go first."

Dash tossed the marble on the floor. It bounced and rolled through the circle and under Ehrich's bed.

"It's okay. You can try again." He held out the last marble.

Dash shrugged.

"You used to love this. I remember one time you won marbles from eight different kids. You took out three with one shot. No one could have pulled that off, not in a million years. The next

Marty Chan

turn, you made the exact same shot. Remember?"

The younger Weisz stared at the floor, saying nothing.

"Dash, help me out here. Do you remember this? Do you remember anything?"

His gaze remained focused on the floor. Ehrich reluctantly picked up the marbles and put them back in his pocket.

"What about the stew Mother used to cook?" he said, trying to get a response from Dash. "That was the best thing to eat on a cold Sunday afternoon. She left the peel on the potatoes because she knew you loved the taste of them."

Dash gritted his teeth and clenched his fists.

"You always tipped the bowl up so you could finish the broth, and it dribbled down your chin onto the table. She slapped you on the back of the head when you tried to slurp the dregs off the table."

"Shut up, shut up, shut up. Shut up!" Dash curled up on his bed.

"What's wrong, Dash?"

Barely audible, his brother murmured, "Remembering hurts."

Ehrich's chest tightened. Dash's pain almost radiated from his body in waves. He desperately wanted to stop his brother's pain, but he believed there was only one way to do this. Get him home.

•—◦◦◦◦—•

Later that evening, the allies convened in Mr. Serenity's quarters. Tesla lounged on the divan looking over the shoulder of Mr. Serenity, as he examined sketches of the Infinity Coil. About the size of a hand, the copper medallion contained a myriad of interlocking gears on one side. The gears seemed to descend deep into the heart of the medallion with no end.

On the other side of the Infinity Coil, the image of a lion with a goat's head on its back and a snake instead of a tail stared out. The rotund man leafed through the sketches of this mysterious artefact.

Amina entered the room, pulling off her heavy wool overcoat. Ehrich greeted her from the table. He picked the last bits of lime green pulp from the rind of an exotic fruit, leaving only a few morsels on the plate.

"Ah, good. I'm starving."

Tesla glanced up. "Did you find anyone willing to keep watch above?"

She sat down at the table beside Ehrich and rummaged for bits to eat among the near-empty plates. "The soldiers don't want to give up any of their trainees. And the civilians who aren't training, well, they look like they'd blow over in the wind. I took what I could get. What's left to eat?"

"My apologies, Amina," Tesla said. "We were famished."

She shook her head. "You must have a hollow leg to store all that food you eat."

Mr. Serenity laughed. "Take it easy on the man, Amina. He's barely skin and bones. He needs some meat on those ribs."

"I wouldn't need to eat so much if someone shared the burden of watching the tunnel."

Mr. Serenity held up the sketches. "I have my priorities."

"Ah, yes. I see your drawing skills have not yet improved."

The two chuckled.

"None of you is taking this seriously. Ole Lukoje is at large. We don't know if all of Ba Tian's generals are in custody. Who knows where Ba Tian is? We have to prepare for war. There are weapons within our reach if we take the initiative."

"Perhaps there is another alternative," Mr. Serenity said. "I've been thinking about our predicament, and I believe we are going about this the wrong way."

"There is no other way," Amina said.

"Let's assume for a moment that the exoskeletons are the linchpin between victory and failure. Ideally, we want to control them but, failing that, we need to keep them out of Ba Tian's hands. Correct?"

She tilted her head to one side. Ehrich shifted forward, curious. Tesla smiled and nodded his head. "Conductors and insulators?"

Mr. Serenity beamed. "Exactly."

"Um, does someone want to put that in English?"

Tesla turned to Ehrich. "Right now, the exoskeletons are conductors, metaphorically speaking. In other words, my generator is a conductor that allows electric currents to flow; in this case, the exoskeletons as conductors could bring the war to an end quickly, depending on who possessed them."

Mr. Serenity stood up. "And we've always associated them with Ba Tian, which was why everyone feared the warlord."

"But could we use them to decimate his forces?" Amina asked.

"Perhaps, by turning the exoskeletons into metaphoric insulators, we can use them to resist Ba Tian."

Ehrich shook his head. "That would take too much time, and we'd create a new enemy. Imagine the panic among the New Yorkers if they saw these machines lumbering down their streets. Do you want to fight a war on two fronts?"

Tesla added. "You raise a good point. Tensions are already high and we don't have enough time. The appearance of these machines would push people over the edge."

A creak distracted Ehrich. He glanced around the room for the source. The door was slightly ajar. He walked over and shut it.

"What if no one possessed the machines?" Ehrich suggested.

Amina straightened up. "We might have a fighting chance."

"And we wouldn't turn the people of my dimension against you," Tesla added.

"Exactly." Mr. Serenity said.

"How do we take the exoskeletons out of the picture?" Ehrich asked.

"The machines are housed under thousands of tons of earth," Mr. Serenity said. "We could collapse the tunnel. I might be able to devise an explosive device, but we would need to plant it underground."

"So we're back to square one." Amina crossed her arms over her chest.

Tesla shook his head. "Not necessarily. It would certainly be easier to get a few people past the defenses with an explosive device than to get a troop to retrieve the exoskeletons."

"We can't afford to wait," Amina declared. "We can't be sure which of Ba Tian's generals are still at large."

Tesla stroked his chin. "He requires the nano-dust, the particles that he used to jump between dimensions. I believe Thomas Edison's hunters confiscated the material from Ole Lukoje when they had him in custody. Most likely, the nano-dust is in Mr. Edison's laboratory."

Ehrich straightened up. "If we get the dust, I can get home."

"Unless Ole Lukoje has it already," Amina said.

Mr. Serenity drummed his fingers on his belly. "So many variables. Did he retrieve the nano-dust? If he did, why would he still be here?"

"I'm betting my life he's in New York," Ehrich said. "If we could talk to someone in Demon Watch, we might find out if the nano-dust is secure."

"I don't think we have any allies left," Tesla said. "We had Charlie, but we know what happened to him."

"Charlie? Is that the boy in the coma?" Mr. Serenity asked.

Ehrich stared down at his plate. Guilt began to punch at his stomach, threatening to bring up the dinner he had just eaten. He recalled how Charlie had risked his life to save him and Ehrich had repaid him by using his unconscious body as bait to lure Kifo out. He hated himself for what he had done.

"We have no other options. That's why we need to get into the tunnel," Amina said. "For all we know, Ba Tian's generals are already down there."

Tesla rubbed his belly. "I'm with Mr. Serenity on this, Amina. If Ba Tian's soldiers secured the exoskeletons, all of New York would know it. Without Ba Tian and the generals, whatever army is left here would have gone into hiding."

"What if Ole Lukoje uses the nano-dust to summon Ba Tian's army?" Amina asked.

Ehrich shook his head. "I saw his technology in action. I think he can only transport one or two people at a time."

"Then what if he jumps into Demon Gate? Gets there and opens the portal for Ba Tian's remaining forces in the other dimensions?"

"You're assuming he'd still be loyal to Ba Tian," Ehrich pointed out. "I think Ole Lukoje is more of a survivor. Without Ba Tian, he'd look out for himself."

Tesla nodded. "Besides, opening a second portal in Demon Gate would be an unwise move."

"Why?" Amina asked.

"I've seen what happens when someone attempts to open another dimensional portal near the Demon Gate. A traveller came through one time with a device and set it off by accident."

"Tell us what happened, my friend," Mr. Serenity urged.

"The two fields ripped the fabric of time and space. Whoever was caught in the distortion vortex was torn apart. It took the hunters two weeks to clean up the mess, but they never could quite get rid of the odour."

Ehrich stood up. "Our best plan of action is to track down Ole Lukoje and his nano-dust. That will get Dash and me home."

Amina crossed her arms. "Waste of time, Ehrich. We need to destroy the exoskeletons."

"The war is over."

"Not for me!"

Mr. Serenity placed his beefy hand on Amina's shoulder. "We should save our fighting for the enemy. Not each other."

Tesla backed him up. "I agree. Let's take a moment to consider what options we have."

Ehrich and Amina said nothing. The tension in the air was thick. Mr. Serenity walked to the counter, picked up a china teapot, and poured steaming liquid into bone-white cups at the oval table. "I think some tea might be in order."

"Fragrant," Tesla said, trying to ease the tension. "Which world did you get this from?"

"I can't remember. Amina would. Can you tell us?"

She shambled to the table and leaned over the steaming pot to sniff. "Rizenberries from Saltzenwendt."

Mr. Serenity smiled. "Ah, yes. Good nose. I remember the peddler from that dimension. She spoke highly of their beverages."

"Well, I do hope we can find more of this tea," Tesla said.

Mr. Serenity fell silent.

"Did I say something wrong?"

"Salzenwendt fell to Ba Tian's forces. There's nothing but scorched earth there now," Amina said.

They sipped their tea in silence. Ehrich stared at his cup. An idea formed like the swirl of cream expanding in the tea. He looked up.

"Kifo worked with Ole Lukoje. They were in contact with each other. He would know Ole Lukoje's hiding spots."

"Yes, but Kifo is dead," Amina pointed out.

Ehrich recalled his hand in the death of the assassin. Kifo had possessed Ning Shu, Ba Tian's daughter, who had rebelled against her father and joined Ehrich's group. As Ning Shu, Kifo was able to take command of the generals on the *Oriental Clipper* airship. Ehrich's group had fought the generals and soldiers for control of the airship. In the battle, Kifo had died in Ning Shu's body. Though they had lost a valuable ally, they had defeated the assassin and recovered the Infinity Coil.

"We don't know exactly how the medallion works, but what if there's a connection between Kifo and all the souls he took? Maybe they could read or hear his thoughts. What if they know what he knew? We could reach out to Ning Shu in the Infinity Coil. Ask if she can tell us where Ole Lukoje might be hiding."

Mr. Serenity scratched his earlobe, thinking: "The Infinity Coil is a storehouse of the souls. I suppose we might be able to communicate with the spirits within."

Tesla disagreed. "How could we even be sure the souls are still in there?"

"We could talk to Dash about his experiences."

Ehrich stiffened. "Have you see him recently? He's a wreck. We push him any further, he'll snap. Promise me you will not involve him."

Tesla patted Ehrich on the shoulder. "We will leave him out of it."

"Could we release Ning Shu from the Infinity Coil?" Amina asked.

"Her body's under the river. Probably half eaten by the fish," Ehrich said. "There's no way to reunite her mind with her body."

"Perhaps a surrogate body," Tesla suggested.

"Any volunteers?" Amina asked.

No one answered.

Mr. Serenity stood up. "Right now, it's merely a theory. Let's adjourn for the evening and muse on the idea. Perhaps inspiration will strike us by morning."

"Good idea, my friend." Tesla stood up.

Amina growled. "We'd better not wait too long."

Mr. Serenity patted her on the shoulder. "Trust me, Amina. I know the urgency of all of this."

The group parted ways. Ehrich headed down the hallway to his quarters. He stopped as he neared the door. It was ajar. He peered inside the room. Dash rested on his side, asleep, except he still wore his shoes, which jutted out from under his blanket. Ehrich chewed his bottom lip. Had his brother been spying on them?

AN OLD FRIEND

The next morning, Ehrich, Amina, and two new recruits from Purgatory headed to the surface of New York to take a shift on the watch at the Hudson River tunnel. The journey through the pneumatic tubes tested the constitution of the volunteers. One nearly vomited when the sled pulled into the docking station in a shop cellar. Amina could see why the soldiers opted to leave this pair out of the training, but beggars couldn't be choosers.

Amina marched up the stairs to the street. She nodded at the gatekeeper, a traveller posing as an oyster merchant, whose cart was strategically placed in front of the cellar doors. Ehrich took up the rear, inhaling the smell of the fresh oysters as he emerged. He grinned at the heavyset gatekeeper and reached for a shell.

She slapped his hand away and growled, "No money, no food. Get on your way."

Ehrich rubbed his hand and thought she was playing the part of a surly vendor far too well. He followed Amina and the recruits to the Hudson River. The emaciated pair looked as if they would be more comfortable in a hospital ward than on the streets of New York. The older one parted her long black hair from her forehead to reveal a third eye. Her younger companion—the mouse-like man who had vomited—stared bewilderedly at the scene around them. Ehrich thought they might cry at any minute.

"The important thing to do is to blend in with everyone else," Amina said. "Don't draw any attention to yourself. Watch for Ba Tian's soldiers. If you see any crimson travellers, Elba, you will return to Purgatory and tell us. Renata will follow the soldiers. Mark an arrow on the ground every few paces so we can track you. Understood?"

The recruit with the third eye accepted the chalk from Amina. The nervous one, Elba, gaped at the fence and travellers, shuffling from one foot to the other.

"We'll stay with you for the first couple of hours until you settle in."

Ehrich patted Elba on the shoulder. "You'll do fine."

"And if you see any weak spots in the fence security, report that as well," Amina said. "Now, find a vantage point and plant yourselves."

They shuffled down the street.

"Do you think they'll be able to handle this?" Ehrich asked. "I think they'll bolt at the sight of an alley cat."

"Let's see if we can convince some of the travellers to help us."

"Actually, I was thinking about the break-in at Edison's Orange County facilities. It's a long shot, but I might be able to track Ole Lukoje if I can talk to the guards at the facilities."

"You think you can find him?"

"I was a demon hunter, Amina. Tracking was my job. I'll start at Edison's Orange County facility and ask about the break-in."

"And now you're a fugitive. I doubt anyone is going to volunteer any information to you."

He stroked his goatee. "Not me, but I'm sure they'll be more than willing to talk to Mr. Edison's director of dimensional acquisitions."

"A ruse? Risky, Ehrich. Too risky."

"It's worth the risk if I can find him. What do you say?"

"It's a long shot at best."

"But it's better than just waiting." He nodded at the recruits, who leaned awkwardly against a wall and stared at the travellers nearby.

Amina sighed. "Go on. I'm going to have to mind these two longer than I thought."

"Thanks, Amina. I'll get back as soon as I learn anything."

"I wouldn't complain if you found some lunch on your way back."

"I'll see what I can do."

—◦WW◦—

Ehrich jogged away from the Hudson River and headed to Edison's laboratory. He found a coach headed toward the county and paid his fare. As the horse-drawn coach rattled across the roads, he stared at the passing terrain. The city streets were his new home, but when the coach rolled into the countryside, the pastures and forests reminded Ehrich of his real home. He longed to return with his brother, wondering how their parents had fared in their absence. Did they think the brothers had run away? Did they fear something evil had befallen them? And how would they react to the brothers' return?

Ehrich imagined his mother's arms wrapping around him, and he could almost feel his father's strong hand clap on his shoulder. In his fantasy, he saw Dash's face light up and his kid brother return to his former self, instead of the hollow and sullen boy that he was now.

Two hours later, he arrived at the laboratory. Hunters were posted at the gate. Ehrich checked his disguise and approached the sentries.

"Morning," he greeted them.

The two females grunted at him, narrowing their gaze. "What's your business here?"

"Commissioner Edison sent me to check on the facility," Ehrich said. "He wanted me to inventory the items inside."

The freckle-faced hunter cocked her head. "Word travels fast. It wasn't our fault."

Ehrich played dumb. "Your fault for what?"

"The break-in. That's why you're here, isn't it?"

"Of course. Yes. Why would you think Edison is blaming you?"

"We heard rumours."

"Don't worry. He hasn't mentioned anything about you. He just wanted to know what was taken."

"That's the weird thing. We don't think anything was taken."

The taller girl interrupted. "Well, that's not quite true. Karen's eyes."

The freckle-faced girl looked down. "Yes. Right."

Ehrich probed. "The thief took her eyes?"

The hunters nodded in unison. "I don't know how she

survived, but she's no use to Edison anymore."

"Where is Karen now?" he asked.

"I think they sent her to a convalescent home. Somewhere in the Bowery."

Ehrich stiffened. The home where Charlie was. His guilt began to gnaw at him again. "Thanks. I guess I'll be on my way."

"You're not going in?" the taller girl asked, narrowing her gaze.

"You said it yourself. Nothing was taken. It came at a dear cost, but I'll tell Mr. Edison you did your jobs."

The hunters relaxed and smiled. The freckle-faced one said, "Yes, tell him that. Ask if he can take us off this guard duty and give us patrol work."

"I'll see what I can do."

He waved as he left, thinking that Karen might give him the answers he needed. He headed to the Bowery and the home where Charlie was staying. Part of him dreaded going because of the guilt that gnawed at him for using his friend's body as bait. Still, he needed answers.

It was mid-afternoon by the time he arrived in the Bowery. Dingy handwritten signs in windows replaced bright shop awnings along the cobblestone streets. The brick buildings showed wear and tear from the train pollution. Gone were the ladies and gentlemen in their Fifth Avenue finery; now middle-class workers in drab outfits drifted or loitered in the streets. Ehrich spotted pickpockets circling around an innocent victim. Prostitutes flashed their skirts at him. He turned away, embarrassed.

Finally, he arrived at a street that no one frequented, not even the toughest thug. The only people who came here were the ones who had lost everything, including hope and fear. At the end of the road sat a nursing home. This was the convalescent home where Charlie lived and where Karen had been sent.

Ehrich stepped onto the porch, debating whether to knock on the door. He pressed his hand against his fake goatee and moustache then knocked. The door opened. Inside the door stood a thin-framed vision of beauty: Bess. She looked exactly as she had when Ehrich first flirted with her when he'd posed as Harry Houdini in the shabby Bijou Theatre. He almost hugged her until he remembered the last time he'd seen her was when he'd tied her up to be left to the mercy of the hunters. She'd had some choice words for him when they parted—all of which made him blush.

"Yes? Can I help you?" she asked.

His original plan to pose as a hunter flew out of his mind. He stammered, "S-s-sorry to trouble you, miss, but I think I'm lost. I was told I could find the haberdashery on this street."

He feared she'd see through his disguise, but she merely furrowed her lovely brow. "A haberdashery? I can't think of one in the neighbourhood."

"Oh. I suspect the young men who gave me the information might have bamboozled me."

Bess laughed. "They're most likely waiting with clubs to bash your brains in so they can take your money."

"Oh, dear. I wanted to get some mending done. I'll leave you and be on my way." He started to back away from the porch.

"What do you need fixed? Maybe I can help."

"You're too kind, but I've taken up enough of your time, miss."

"Nonsense. I could use a distraction. Show me what you need mended."

Ehrich tipped his hat with a grand flourish, misdirecting Bess so he could rip something from his jacket. He held up a black button: "It came loose when I woke and managed to unravel itself through the morning. I don't want to trouble you … miss?"

"Call me Bess. And you are?"

"My name is Blackstone," Ehrich answered.

"Well, come in, before the thieves come for your money," she said, stepping aside.

He entered, catching a hint of her fresh-scented hair as he passed by. A mahogany table occupied the space by the hallway wall, right under a gilded mirror. In the sitting room, an Oriental rug covered the hardwood floor and a large armoire sat against the far wall. Indented wheel tracks marked the rug.

"Do you live here by yourself?" he asked.

She shook her head. "No, I work here."

"What do you do?"

"I'm a pusher of chairs."

Ehrich cocked his head to one side, feigning ignorance.

She laughed. "I look after the patients who live here."

"Patients?"

She noted the wall of black-and-white photos. All of them featured people in wheelchairs. Some stared directly at the camera with fierce defiance. Others gaped vacantly.

"They have no families to look after them. Well, no families that will take responsibility, anyway. The state sent them here to live out what years they have left."

"And you tend to them all?" Ehrich asked.

"Well, me and Mrs. Sherman. She runs the home. Are you going to take that off?" she asked.

"Excuse me?"

"Did you think I would sew your button on while you were still wearing the jacket?"

"Oh, right," Ehrich said. He began to take off his jacket. "Is this your main occupation? Looking after the patients?"

"No. In my spare time, I mend jackets for strangers."

He chuckled. "Thank you. I appreciate this. How many patients do you have?"

"Right now, we're tending to eight. No, seven."

"Oh?"

"The new one, well, she didn't make it. Lost her eyes and her spirit to go on."

Ehrich's heart sank. His one lead to Ole Lukoje was gone.

"Well, this looks easy to fix. Just a matter of how much you need it mended."

"What?"

"How much are you willing to pay?"

"Oh. Of course," Ehrich said. "How much for your services?"

"Five cents. You should learn how to sew, Blackstone. Might save you some money in the future."

"Then I'd put you out of work."

Bess laughed as she perched on a hard bench near the window. She pulled a needle and thread from a sewing box. He wondered if she missed the footlights and the audiences of the Bijou Theatre—maybe not the catcalls or the theatre owner's wandering hands. He wondered if she still performed or if she cared about the Harry Houdini act anymore.

A series of knocks from upstairs shook him out of his reverie.

"Is your employer upstairs?" he asked.

"No. It's one of my patients. He's a handful." She looked up and called out, "What do you want, Charlie?!"

Ehrich stiffened. Charlie? Awake? Questions flooded his mind. Charlie's voice called back. "I'm thirsty."

"I'll get you water in a minute."

"I'm really thirsty."

She sighed and set the jacket down. Ehrich waved her off. "No, I can do it."

"Now you're doing my job."

"I don't mind. Call it a fair trade."

"You still have to pay."

"I will, but now you'll owe me something in return."

"Thank you. You'll find a pitcher of fresh lemonade in the kitchen. Take a left off the hallway."

Ehrich entered the kitchen, found the lemonade, and poured a glass. Then he headed upstairs.

"I'm dying of thirst," Charlie cried out from the room at the top of the stairs.

"It's on the way," Bess yelled from below.

Ehrich pushed the bedroom door open. He stifled a gasp at the sight of his old friend sitting upright in a narrow bed. The shock of blond hair was longer and his face was gaunt, but he was alive and alert.

Charlie smiled. "You're new." His voice was hoarse. "You a friend of Bess's?"

"No, a lost traveller. She's mending my jacket and I'm repaying her the kindness. Here." He stepped around the wheelchair sitting in front of the bed and passed Charlie the glass of lemonade.

"Thanks. My name's Charlie. Who do I have the pleasure of speaking to?"

"Blackstone. Nice to meet you."

Charlie sipped the lemonade. "Ah. That's good. Do we know each other?"

Ehrich tapped the side of his leg nervously. "I don't think we've met."

"I ain't so good with faces but I'm damn good with voices, and yours sounds familiar."

Ehrich shook his head. "No one's ever said I had an unforgettable voice. You should hear me sing. That you'll never forget. It will haunt your nightmares."

"I suppose it might."

"So, what happened to you?" Ehrich asked.

"Oh, this. I'll be able to walk eventually, but the muscles need to be built up again. I got into a scrap with some demons. They didn't take too kindly to me."

"Are you all right now?"

"Bess said I was in a coma for a few months, then one day I just woke up."

Ehrich probed a little deeper. "When did that happen?"

"Not sure, really. I guess it was a few months back. Summertime. Weird thing was, when I got up, I thought I was back with my squad mates."

"You worked as a hunter?" Ehrich asked, but he knew the answer.

"Of course I did. Of all people, you should know that, Ehrich."

Ehrich froze.

THE COIL'S CALL

At the Hudson River tunnel project, Amina supervised her recruits. The first hour or so had been tough for them, trying to blend in with the travellers. She nudged the pair to move on when a group of people began staring at them. Now the recruits were settled near the middle section of the fence with a quiet group of women standing around a barrel fire.

Amina then headed to another group of travellers. She sidled up to them. "Any word on when the project will start up again?" she asked.

"Do I look like an official?" a woman with wide eyes asked.

"I thought you might have heard rumours."

"The same stories we hear all the time. They're going to open it when we leave. They're going to put us back to work but only if we agree to work for half as much. They're bringing in people from across the sea to work in the tunnel. They're all just stories."

"How long had you been working in the tunnel?"

"Me? Since they started the project. You?"

"I got the job about a week before it shut down. My name is Amina." She reached out a hand to shake.

"Hexacate," the woman replied, waving it off with her seven-fingered hand.

"Nice to meet you. I don't know how much longer I can wait for the project to start up again. I'm down to picking scraps from the trash for food," Amina said.

"We still have a few supplies. You're welcome to them."

"I don't want to use up your stores. Besides, I've heard there's food if people are willing to do some work for it."

The tall woman leaned in. "Where did you hear this?"

"Around."

"What kind of work?"

"Nothing too hard. Watching the guards on the fence, taking note of their shifts, and any lapses in security."

"Sounds less like work and more like preparing for an assault."

"Interested?"

Hexacate shook her head. "Any battle against the humans isn't going to end well for our kind. They'll have more reasons to kick us out of their dimension. You should tell whoever is offering this work to think twice before they ruin what little chance we have of making peace with the people here."

"Momma, I'm cold." A young boy tugged on Hexacate's skirt.

The burly woman wrapped her arms around the boy. She smiled and walked away with her son. Amina wasn't going to get any help from these travellers. She hoped the others were making progress.

Marty Chan

In Mr. Serenity's laboratory, Nikola Tesla tinkered with the tome-like codex the group had used when they posed as a magic act. On the wall, the projected image of Ehrich as Harry Houdini stepped into a trunk. Tesla adjusted a dial to bring the image into sharper focus. He played with the scale of the image, remembering how they had used this to entertain the Bijou audiences.

Beside him, Mr. Serenity examined the Infinity Coil, scratching his head as he probed at the countless gears within the medallion. He sighed and slapped his tools on the counter.

Tesla glanced over. "Not making any progress, I gather."

"On the surface, this medallion looks like a mechanical marvel, but it's more than gears and sprockets. It's impossible to squeeze that much metal into something that can fit in my hand, yet it exists. It's a paradox."

Tesla moved closer and examined the Infinity Coil mounted between the clamps. The intricate designs along the medallion's perimeter appeared to be infinity symbols, but what fascinated Tesla was the endless network of gears on the front of the medallion, which overlapped each other and descended far deeper into the copper-coloured device than they should have been able to.

Mr. Serenity asked, "Have you ever seen the likes of this kind of device?"

"This is beyond anything I could have even dreamed of. The gears are powered through no motor that I can see."

"And yet they are in perpetual motion." Mr. Serenity noted the precise ticking movements of the gears. Some rotated clockwise. Others moved counter clockwise. But they all moved in sync with each other.

"If we are to see how this device works, it only makes sense to separate it into its corresponding components."

"I suppose you are right, Tesla." The rotund man picked up a pair of tweezers and a thin metal probe. He inserted the probe between the cogs of one of the larger gears near the top of the medallion. The gear continued to rotate. He applied more pressure but couldn't stop the machine.

"What's wrong, Mr. Serenity?"

"I'm not sure, but it seems the gears are stronger than I thought."

"Let me help," Tesla offered. He picked up another metal probe, about the width of a pencil lead and inserted it through the spoke of the gear Mr. Serenity was trying to stop. His eyes widened when the instrument recoiled from the contact, like the two positive ends of a magnet repelling each other. At the same moment, Mr. Serenity's instrument snapped. The tip flew off and skittered across the lab table.

"Curious," Mr. Serenity said. "Perhaps we'll need something non-ferrous."

"And something a bit sturdier."

The bigger man rubbed his chin. "Vezium is the strongest metal that existed in my world. It would be like the iron you have in this world but 50 times stronger."

"Well, then, I wish we could get our hands on some."

Mr. Serenity held up the broken end of his instrument. "I did."

Tesla's eyes widened.

Mr. Serenity drummed his fingers on his worktable. "I have a device that can scan the internal workings of machines without pulling them apart."

"Intriguing. What do you call your device?"

"A radiographometer." Mr. Serenity beamed as he stepped to

the far end of the room to roll a large boxy machine with glass tubes along the top and copper tubes throughout the mainframe. He attached the codex to the top of the box. "This will show us what the device sees." He rolled the machine to the counter with the Infinity Coil until the two were nearly touching. He pulled a lever on the machine. Diodes began to flash. The glass tubes filled with smoke. He motioned Tesla to step back.

A powerful beam of green light bathed the medallion. The codex lens sparked to life and projected the image of the Infinity Coil against the far wall. Mr. Serenity adjusted a lever on the radiographometer and the image inverted in colour from white to black. To Tesla's surprise, tiny ghostly faces appeared on the surface of the medallion. They began to expand from the Infinity Coil to fill the entire screen. The faces of men, women, and children bobbed on the screen like flotsam on top of the ocean.

Mr. Serenity scratched his head. "I don't understand. We should be seeing the inside of the Infinity Coil. Gears, mechanisms."

"My friend, I think we are seeing the true coil. The gears are what we perceive on the outside, but these are the souls of the people trapped within."

"That's impossible."

"The Infinity Coil defies explanation, Mr. Serenity. I want to say it's mechanical, but I think the device is just as much mystical."

"Magic. I can't subscribe to that, Nikola, and surely you can't, either."

"Advanced technology will seem like magic until the secrets are unlocked. When I first proposed the idea of conducting electricity without copper wires, people thought I was insane."

Suddenly, the faces twisted in agony and uttered silent

screams. The people in the image almost appeared to be the tortured prisoners of Dante's *Inferno.*

Mr. Serenity turned off the machine and the images faded out.

"This is beyond anything I could imagine. I can't begin to explain half of this," Tesla said.

"I think I know who might," replied Mr. Serenity. "Dash."

Tesla shook his head. "The boy's fragile and I'm not certain if he has any inkling of the inner workings of the Infinity Coil."

"But he is the only one who has experienced the power of the medallion."

"We promised Ehrich we would not involve Dash."

"I'm merely suggesting a few probing general questions to give us some direction on how to proceed. Surely there can be no harm in asking him a question or two."

"I suppose not, but can we do it after lunch?"

Mr. Serenity chuckled as he ushered his friend out of the lab. "My friend, you're always hungry. How on Earth do you manage to stay slim with an appetite like that?"

"Constitutional walks are the key."

"Let's bring Dash. The boy could use a hot meal and some company. I think he is homesick. I've seen that mood in the other refugees in Purgatory. Solitude does not improve the mood. However, breaking bread with comrades provides a welcome distraction."

"A good point, especially if that bread is the tetraz cake in the marketplace."

Mr. Serenity clapped his friend on the back and they headed out of the chambers. They arrived at the Weisz brothers' quarters and Tesla knocked on the door. No answer. He knocked again.

"Dash?"

Still nothing. Mr. Serenity pushed the door open. The room was empty.

"Dash! Hello? That's odd. Where could the boy have gone to?"

Mr. Serenity walked down the hallway. "Let's check the other rooms."

They walked along the hallway to Amina's room. The place was in shambles. Clothes were strewn across the floor and old half-eaten sandwiches sat on top of the unmade bed. She was a mighty warrior and a lousy housekeeper.

They moved to Tesla's room. In contrast to Amina's mess, his room was impeccably neat. Not even a hair would have been found anywhere among the neatly stacked clothes on the dresser.

"Do you think he went outside?" Mr. Serenity asked.

"You suggested he was homesick. Perhaps he's looking for something familiar."

"In Purgatory? What could that be?"

"Nothing here that I can think of. What about the surface?" Tesla asked. "You don't think he ran away, do you?"

They hustled to the docking station of the pneumatic tube transport system. One bay was empty while a sled was parked in the other one. Mr. Serenity scratched his head. "Amina and Ehrich took one to the surface, so there's no way Dash could have gone up this way. Where could he have gone?"

"I don't know."

They returned to Mr. Serenity's chambers. As they entered, Tesla noticed the door to the lab was wide open. He glanced at Mr. Serenity and then glanced at the open door. His companion inched along the wall and picked up a lamp from a nearby table to use as a weapon. He inched to the doorway with Tesla behind him.

The two men peeked into the doorway, then Mr. Serenity shoved the door open and jumped into the lab. He waved the lamp at the intruder within—Dash. The young Weisz was trying to pry the Infinity Coil from the clamps.

"Stop!" Mr. Serenity said. "What are you doing?"

The boy withdrew his hands and stuck them behind his back. "Nothing."

Tesla came out from behind Mr. Serenity. "You know you're not supposed to be in here by yourself."

"I'm sorry," Dash said.

Mr. Serenity walked over and examined the medallion. It was still safely moored in the clamps. "Why were you trying to take the Infinity Coil?"

"I wasn't," he said.

"Easy, Dash," Tesla said. "You know this is a dangerous artefact."

"I know how dangerous it is. It's ruined my life." He stormed out of the lab before Tesla could stop him.

Mr. Serenity turned to his friend. "Do you think he wanted to steal it or destroy it?"

"I don't know, but I think I'd better find out what's bothering the boy."

SURPRISE VISIT

"**H**ow did you know?" Ehrich asked, self-consciously pressing his fingers against his fake goatee.

Charlie chuckled. "You expect people only to look at your face, but a hunter notices everything. I've been your partner long enough to recognize your nervous tic. Tapping your leg. Then there's the way you speak."

"I lowered my voice."

"You can't hide the rhythm of your speech or the way your eyes shift around the room. You can take the guy out of the hunter but you can't take the hunter out of the guy. That spider on your face real or did you grow it?"

Ehrich laughed. "Fake. I'm relieved that you're no longer in the coma."

"Yeah? Bess said my body made pretty good bait."

"What did she tell you?"

"Weird story. She claimed a Dimensional could possess

people, and you tried to trick him into taking over my body to trap him inside me."

"I didn't know if you were ever going to come out of the coma."

"So you assumed I was going to be thrilled with being used as a meat puppet."

Ehrich raised his hands. "I know it was wrong, and I can't ever expect that you'd forgive me, but I needed to catch this assassin."

"Ehrich, you nearly wiped me out forever."

"If there's anything I could do to make it up to you, I would."

"You want to make it up to me?"

"Yes. What can I do?"

Charlie beckoned him closer. "You know what you could do for me?"

"Yes? What?"

"I'd kill for a steak and some potatoes. I'd even settle for fresh oysters and hot yams." Charlie broke into a grin and laughed. "I had you on the line. The colour left your face faster than a cat shoots out of a rain barrel. Oh, man, you were squirming."

"So you're not mad at me?"

"Oh, I'm spittin' mad. Never came to visit me when I regained consciousness. What kind of friend are you?"

"I didn't know. When did you wake up?"

"A week after you pulled that stunt. The doctor can't explain it, but I think it was something you did. In a way, I owe you my life, but you're still a bad friend for not visiting."

Ehrich cracked a grin. "How do you know I didn't drop by when you were in a coma? Maybe I was here every day."

Charlie laughed. "What were you doing? Showing me card tricks? Pick a card. Any card."

"Yeah, and I found your card every time."

"Oh, man, thank goodness for the coma. I didn't have to hear your patter. Why are you here now, Ehrich?"

"I felt bad about what I did. I wanted to see if you were feeling better."

"I'm fit as a fiddle with broken strings." He tapped his legs. "So all this cloak and dagger stuff, have you caught the one you were looking for?"

"I think we did, but he has allies. I'm looking for one of them."

"Anything I can do to help?"

"You remember that Dimensional I tracked when I was on Demon Watch? The one who took people's eyes?"

Charlie narrowed his gaze. "Dangerous one. Yeah. You don't forget someone like that very quickly. Not when you've seen his victims. What about him?"

"I think he might still be at large. I need to know if he tried to get into any of Thomas Edison's laboratories."

Charlie shook his head. "Ehrich, you are a terrible liar. You expect me to believe that you came all the way down here to talk to a guy in a coma about a Dimensional? Do you take me for a fool?"

"Sorry? I don't know what you're going on about, Charlie."

"Ehrich, it's been my experience that someone who goes to these lengths to see a girl has something else on his mind. You're here to see Bess."

Ehrich felt his face flush. "Am not."

"I can tell when you're lying."

"I think I liked you better when you were in a coma." He tapped his fingers against the side of his leg.

"You're sweet on her, Ehrich. The fingers never lie."

Ehrich stopped tapping. "You have the wrong idea, Charlie."

"Blackstone!" Bess called from below. "Your button is mended."

"Here's your chance, Ehrich. Go tell her how you feel."

"I'm not. You're wrong. I can't. She's just ... Never mind."

"Good luck, pal. Just watch out for her right hook. She packs a mean punch when she's mad."

Ehrich lingered for a moment then headed out of the room.

"Good to see you, Charlie."

"Next time, bring a steak with all the trimmings."

Ehrich smiled and closed the door. He headed downstairs. In the parlour, Bess held up the jacket for him to examine. He pretended to survey her work but peeked through the arm of the jacket at the lovely girl in the parlour. He wondered if Charlie was right. Bess was the one person who made this world feel less alien. She made him feel like he was at home. Part of him wanted to tell Bess everything. Another part wanted to keep silent.

"I'm impressed, Bess. Nice work."

"I've had enough wardrobe emergencies in my dance troupe to get familiar with a needle and thread." She smiled at him. He missed that smile so much.

"Actually, I have something to talk to you about, Bess."

She put away her needle and thread in a wooden box. "Oh?"

"The truth is, Bess, my name's not Blackstone."

"You're free to use whatever name you want. I'm not judging."

"I thought you should know the truth." He tugged the goatee off his chin. He then removed his spectacles.

Bess's eyes widened. "You!"

"Let me explain."

The wooden box flew at him. He ducked instinctively as it smashed against the wall behind him. Bess grabbed a poker from the fireplace and brandished it like a club.

"I'm not letting you tie me up again!"

"Lower the poker. I'm not here to hurt you."

She waved the poker in his face, angling herself toward the hallway.

"I never meant to tie you up. That was part of the group's plan. We were desperate to escape and we—they—didn't know if we could trust you."

"Do you know how many hours I spent being interrogated by Thomas Edison and his hunters? The months of checking over my shoulder for hunters following me because they thought I was off to meet with you?"

"I'm sorry, Bess." He took a step forward.

She waved the poker, forcing him back. "Once Godfrey learned I might have been an accomplice, he fired me. He didn't even pay me for the two weeks I had already worked. He left me high and dry. The other members of my dance troupe wouldn't even talk to me. They treated me like I was a leper. And it's all thanks to you."

A knock on the door. Ehrich froze. Bess could call for help and it would all be over.

"Who is it?" she asked.

"Elizabeth and Jennifer."

"They're hunters," Bess whispered. "Hide in the kitchen."

Ehrich raised an eyebrow. Why was Bess helping him? No time to argue. He ran to the kitchen and skidded to a halt. There was no back door and the window was too small to squeeze through. She had trapped him. He pressed his back against the wall and eavesdropped.

The front door opened. "Afternoon," a girl's voice said.

All Bess needed to do was blow his cover. One scream would do it. He held his breath.

Bess said a little too brightly, "Elizabeth. Jennifer. What brings you by so soon?"

"We decided to visit Charlie early. We might not have the chance later."

"Why?"

"Shifts are changing."

"You mean doubling," the other girl complained.

"Well, Charlie will be happy for the company. I'll take you up."

Footsteps echoed. Ehrich waited a few minutes then peeked into the hallway. Bess had left the front door open. He could flee into the street without anyone being the wiser, but he stopped at the bottom of the steps. Why were the shifts doubling?

Curious, he crept up the stairs. Charlie's door was closed. Ehrich tiptoed to one side and listened.

"You can't be serious, Elizabeth," Charlie's voice boomed. "Edison wants a public execution?"

"That's the word."

"Why on Earth would he think that's a good idea? Who's going to patrol the streets? Everyone will be pulled for security detail."

"You're preaching to the converted," Elizabeth said. "None of the squad leaders are happy about this, especially with the extra shifts."

"Where is the execution going to be?" Bess asked.

"That's classified," Elizabeth said.

Charlie joked. "Who the heck are we going to tell? The other patients? I'm pretty sure they're not going to gossip."

Bess chimed in. "My lips are sealed."

A pause, then Elizabeth answered: "Coney Island."

"Why a public setting?" Charlie asked. "Hard enough to keep that many prisoners in check, let alone the crowds."

Jennifer piped in. "I think it has to do with the method of the execution. We're not sure, but we've heard rumours that Edison has a new method. Electrocution."

"What does electrocution mean?" Bess asked.

Elizabeth explained, "The word around Devil's Island is that Edison's scientists have figured out a way to harness Tesla's generators to shoot electricity into the body."

"You mean like the Teslatron rifles?" Charlie asked.

"But on a larger scale," Jennifer said. "They're going to fry the prisoners. We heard that if it works, Edison's talking about using it on the other demons."

Ehrich was stunned. He had to get back to Purgatory. He began to make his way out but the floorboard creaked underfoot.

"You hear that?" Elizabeth said.

"Maybe Mrs. Sherman came early today," Bess suggested.

"Jennifer, check on it."

"It's fine," Bess said. "I'll do it."

Footsteps approached the door. Ehrich slipped out of the hallway and down the stairs, two at a time. He reached the bottom and turned around. Bess stood at the top of the stairs. Their eyes locked.

She opened her mouth and whispered, "Go."

He sprinted out of the house. He had to tell the others about the execution.

A MATTER OF TRUST

Purgatory offered its citizens a respite from the horrors of war. The builders had erected a pond at the heart of the underground city. Refugees walked around the shore, amid the flowering shrubs and glowing rocks. Along the perimeter, light towers disguised as trees illuminated the serene park.

At the edge of the water, Tesla barked instructions to Dash: "Wade out. More. More. Good. Now lower the submarine into the water. Slowly."

Dash held a long cylindrical device with no sails. Instead, an antenna jutted up from the midsection of the metal tube. He lowered the craft into the water and it bobbed up and down.

The lanky scientist held a control box about the size of a small book. A tall antenna rose up from the top. Tesla thumbed the two small crank wheels on the face of the device.

"The submarine is moving!" Dash shouted.

"That means it's communicating with my controller. Come

back and I'll let you pilot the craft."

Dash waded back to the shore. Tesla handed him the control box.

"The right wheel controls the direction and the left wheel controls the speed. Get the submarine out to open water first."

Dash smiled as he steered the craft in widening circles.

"Don't send it too far. The range is limited. Think of it as your field of vision. As long as you can see the ship, the signal will reach it."

"Got it." Dash piloted the craft closer to the shore, jumping up and down and laughing as it glided through the water.

A few feet behind them, Ehrich watched in amazement. He hadn't seen his brother like this in a long time. Probably since before they crossed over to this dimension. Seeing Dash act like himself filled Ehrich with happiness. He didn't want to interrupt the moment for fear of chasing away the mood.

Amina grabbed his arm and ordered, "Let's go, Ehrich. We have to tell Tesla."

She had been itching to reveal Ehrich's discovery ever since he reported to her at the Hudson River.

"Sir, sir. We have to talk," she called as she ran to the shore.

"Ah, Ehrich. Amina. Good to see you both back."

"Mr. Tesla, we have to talk," Amina said.

"In a moment. Dash, see if you can pilot the submarine through those reeds."

Dash laughed as he steered the vessel through the plants jutting out of the water.

"How are you controlling that thing?" Ehrich asked.

Dash beamed as he held up the control box.

"Amazing. How does it work without wires?"

Tesla tapped the antenna. "My controller sends a radio signal through this to the antenna attached to the submarine."

"It's a remote control," Dash said.

"I like that name, Dash. I think we'll use it."

Ehrich pulled Tesla aside and whispered, "How did you get him to smile?"

"What child doesn't enjoy playing with boats?"

"Incredible," Ehrich said, watching his brother run along the shore to keep up with the floating submarine. He began to follow but Amina grabbed his shirt.

"That can wait. Tell Mr. Tesla what you told me."

He reluctantly looked away from his happy brother. "Right. Sir, Thomas Edison is planning to harness your electricity towers to electrocute the prisoners."

"What do you mean 'electrocute'?"

"I overheard hunters talking about it. Electrocution is the word they're using to describe frying the soldiers to death with electricity."

"No, no. That's not why I created the towers. They were supposed to provide efficient energy to households. Not kill men."

"I'm sorry, sir, but that's what I heard."

"My generators were far more efficient than Edison's direct current transformers. I could bring electricity to everyone in the United States. Not just the wealthy. Power for the people who are huddled in tenements in the Bowery. Farmers in the rural areas. Everyone. Rather than listen to me, he decides to discredit my life's work. No one will ever trust AC transformers after this."

"Maybe he's using the execution to lure the rest of Ba Tian's army out of hiding," Amina suggested.

"Possibly," Ehrich said.

"Edison's always envied me. It's not the first time he's savaged his competition. He's ruthless. I will not stand for the perversion of my invention."

"Are you going to jump up on a stage and claim your towers are safe? The hunters will clap you in irons the minute they spot you."

"Where is the execution site?"

Amina answered, "Coney Island."

"We have to go there."

Tesla marched away from the pond. Amina followed him. Ehrich glanced at Dash playing before he chased after the pair.

"If we go in without any plan, we'll end up in prison."

"Ehrich, I can't allow Edison to proceed with this abomination of my work."

"And this might be the perfect chance to finish off any of Ba Tian's forces," Amina added. "If there are any of his generals or soldiers left, they'll be sure to try to stop the execution."

"Wait. Hold on. What if the execution fails?"

Tesla stopped. "Fails? What do you mean, Ehrich?"

"Fizzles out."

"Sabotage?"

"Yes, sir. In front of the public, Edison won't have any choice but to admit he was wrong about your technology."

"He would be beside himself with rage."

"You'll preserve your reputation without Edison suspecting your hand in it."

The lanky scientist smiled. "The perfect revenge."

Later that evening, everyone but Dash gathered in Mr. Serenity's chambers. The younger Weisz was bone tired and headed straight to bed. Ehrich lingered near the open door of the chambers to ensure that Dash wasn't going to eavesdrop on them.

He had good reason to keep an eye out for Dash. Tesla explained the earlier break-in.

"If Mr. Serenity and I hadn't shown up when we did, who knows what Dash would have done with the medallion?"

"I don't understand. What could Dash have done with it?"

"We're not sure if he'd meant to steal it or destroy it," Mr. Serenity pointed out.

Dread washed over Ehrich in waves. "Why would he want the Infinity Coil?" The answer hit him as soon as he asked the question. "Kifo?"

Amina stiffened. "You think he has control of your brother again?"

"We can't be certain either way," Mr. Serenity said. "All we know is that Dash wanted the Infinity Coil."

Tesla added. "You saw your brother at the pond. Do you think Kifo would behave like that?"

"To throw off any suspicion, he would," Amina said.

"I don't know," Ehrich said. "He seemed like his old self at the pond, but I also thought he was spying on us the other night. His behaviour is erratic at best."

"Until we are certain one way or the other, it may be best to keep an eye on Dash," Amina concluded.

Ehrich reeled from the possibility that his brother was still trapped. He had spent years searching for him, only to learn Kifo had possessed the boy's body. His chest tightened. Through gritted teeth, he declared, "How can we find out?"

Mr. Serenity nodded to Tesla. "Earlier, Nikola and I discovered a way to examine the Infinity Coil."

"The radiographometer," Tesla said. "Yes, we could search for Dash's face among the images."

"It will take time."

"Time is what we don't have," Amina said.

"We will keep the Infinity Coil away from Dash until we know for sure who came back," Mr. Serenity said.

"Wait," Amina said. "Kifo could have taken the Infinity Coil at any time. What's his end game? Do you think he's scouting Purgatory to learn of our defenses?"

"Possibly," Mr. Serenity said. "If so, we might want to remove him."

"No one's touching Dash," Ehrich said.

Tesla patted him on the shoulder. "I think I have a solution. We must scout the execution site for Ba Tian's soldiers. Let's bring Dash with us. Tell the boy we need him as cover."

Amina's eyebrows raised. "Yes, if he's Kifo, he'll lead us to where Ba Tian's forces are hiding."

"If there are any left," Ehrich pointed out.

"Risky move," Mr. Serenity said. "No telling what Dash might do up there."

"Is he more of a threat in Purgatory or in New York? I would rather keep him with me, than have him running loose down here."

Amina agreed. "Mr. Tesla is right. We can keep an eye on him at Coney Island."

"Fine, fine. Are we in agreement?" Mr. Serenity asked.

Ehrich nodded reluctantly.

CONEY ISLAND

Two days later, Ehrich, Tesla, Amina, and Dash boarded a train bound for Coney Island. They had agreed Mr. Serenity would remain in Purgatory to examine the Infinity Coil while the others scouted the execution site. Ehrich concocted the plan to pose as performers, which would give them an excuse to move around the island without raising suspicion.

Dash pressed his face against the window and stared out at the passing buildings. Ehrich secretly watched his brother, wondering who the boy really was. On the seat opposite the Weisz's, Tesla nervously adjusted his tie several times as he stared around the train car, his legs bouncing up and down impatiently. Amina placed her hand on the man's knee and squeezed until the leg went still.

The train steamed across the city, spewing black smoke over the warehouses and tenements adjacent to the elevated tracks. Two women in large bustles sat down across from the group.

They cooled themselves with decorative fans as they chatted casually.

"I'm certain that Mr. Edison will employ a most novel means of execution. After all, he's the man who invented the light bulb," the older woman said.

Her companion nodded. "That invention changed my life. The extra hours at night we have at our home. He is truly a marvel. I can't wait to see what device he'll use to put down those horrid demons."

Ehrich gritted his teeth but said nothing. If the people weren't upset over the travellers in their dimension, they most likely would target another group. The Chinese. The Irish. The African slaves.

When the train reached Coney Island, passengers disembarked. Amina and Tesla unloaded the larger steamer trunk containing their props while the Weisz brothers managed the smaller one.

Ehrich followed the rubberneckers heading to the newly built stage off the boardwalk. Red, white, and blue banners festooned the skirt of the elevated platform. Carpenters worked on the stage, erecting tiered benches at the back. Off to the side, technicians milled about the scattered pieces of scaffolding and machinery. Propped against a crate was a giant doughnut-shaped device wrapped in copper wires.

Tesla gasped. "My generators."

Ehrich stopped and lowered the trunk to the ground and motioned the others to do the same. He checked his fake facial hair. Though they all wore disguises, Ehrich didn't want to take any chances. He'd swapped out his goatee and moustache for a full beard. Tesla had reluctantly agreed to don a fake beard as well, which he constantly scratched at. He strode closer to the stage. Ehrich followed.

Amina lingered back with Dash and the steamer trunks. Her cloak and hood hid her ebony face and scarred arms. Though she could pass for a New Yorker, the scars might raise questions. Dash shifted from foot to foot in his poor-boy cap and suspendered pants and stared at the oddity amidst the construction: an elephant shackled to iron spikes driven into the ground.

Excited gawkers shared their theories with each other. One man claimed, "Edison is going to shoot electricity into the sky and create reverse lightning."

An old man said, "I don't care how he does it. As long as he rids the city of these vile creatures."

Ehrich had heard enough. The crowd gossip wasn't going to help them. He tugged on Tesla's jacket and pulled him back to the steamer trunks.

"Why is there an elephant?" Dash asked.

"I don't know." Ehrich said.

"When do you think they'll stage the execution?" Amina asked.

"Edison will want to test the equipment first," Tesla said. "At the rate the technicians are working, it may be never."

They wandered away from the work site.

—WW—

The execution site wasn't the only attraction on Coney Island. At the far end of the boardwalk, a sideshow tent attracted a small gathering of vacationers. A carnival barker with a smarmy smile and a crooked nose beckoned patrons to enter. "Come one, come all, and marvel at the 'Seven Wonders of the World.' You'll see the world's shortest man. You'll gasp at the Bearded

Lady. You will meet the Seer, the man who can communicate with the great beyond! All for just a nickel. Step right up and see the 'Seven Wonders of the World.'"

A couple walked in and paid the admission. The rest of the crowd moved on to other attractions.

Ehrich headed to the barker.

"Come on in, sir. Just a nickel and you'll see wonders you never imagined."

Ehrich shook his head. "I'm looking for the owner or manager. Who is that?"

The barker tipped his cap at Ehrich. "The name's Bradley Shaw. At your service. Want to step inside and see something you've never witnessed in your life? For you, a nickel."

"I'm hoping to become one of the attractions."

"I have a full slate."

"You won't want to miss this act. I guarantee it will fill your tent."

"Right now, you're chasing away my audience."

"Looks like I'm the only audience you have right now, sir."

Bradley ignored Ehrich and barked at a few bystanders nearby. "Step right up folks. See the Lunatic." He waved at the tent entrance, and two handlers brought out a man with wild eyes and straggly hair. He struggled inside a canvas jacket with his arms crossed over his chest. A line of leather straps along his back from his neck to his bottom were cinched up tightly. He roared at his handlers, frothing at the mouth.

"Plucked from the asylum because he was considered too dangerous, the Lunatic is a wonder to behold. Don't worry, as long as he's in the straitjacket, you'll be safe." Bradley shouted at the tourists, trying to draw them closer. It wasn't working.

Ehrich stepped in front of the stand. "Oh, my goodness! What was that creature? How did he do that amazing thing with his eyes?"

Curious bystanders slowed.

"He's from another dimension. He has to be. I've never see anyone do that before."

Now the people were curious. They approached the tent, eager to look at the Lunatic. Bradley waved at the handlers, who ushered the Lunatic inside. Ehrich smiled at Bradley who ran his finger along his crooked nose as a salute. "Don't take my word for it. This young gentleman saw the Lunatic with his own eyes."

"He's beyond anything I've ever seen. You have to see him to believe it."

The people inched closer to the entrance, fumbling in pockets and purses for the entry fee. They paid and entered. Bradley smiled at Ehrich. "Come back in an hour and show me your act. You'd better knock my socks off."

"We will." Ehrich jogged back to the others to break the good news.

●─\/\/\/─●

An hour later, Ehrich strode onto the wooden stage in the tent. Amina waved her arms in the air to show off the steamer trunk they had placed in the centre of the platform. Bradley sat crossarmed in the front row. Beside him, Dash kicked his legs to and fro staring down at the ground.

On the side of the stage, Tesla clutched the codex and nodded to Ehrich.

"Mr. Shaw, you are in for a delight. Such a feat that you won't be able to tell if it is illusion or pure magic," Ehrich said. "You will wonder if your eyes are truly deceiving you. Take this ordinary steamer trunk."

He kicked the trunk three times, then he and Amina spun it around to show the sides and back were solid. Bradley sighed and motioned Ehrich to hurry up.

"There is only one way in or out." He opened the lid and climbed into the trunk. Amina wrapped chains over the top of the trunk and locked them to the front. When the trunk was secured, she lifted a hoop draped with black material, circled the stage, and stepped on top of the trunk. She lifted the hoop over her head. A pause, then the hoop dropped. Ehrich now stood alone on top of the trunk. Amina had disappeared. On the side of the stage, Tesla aimed the Codex at the steamer trunk.

Bradley yawned. "That all you got? Every magician in town is doing 'Metamorphosis.'"

Ehrich straightened up. "But we do it differently."

"Guy goes in the box, girl comes out. That's the basic plot, right? I've seen them all. Girl goes in, guy comes out. Guy goes in, comes out in different clothes. Girl goes in and a kid comes out. Trust me, I've seen every variation of this act since Harry Houdini introduced this trick."

Ehrich fought the urge to smile. He wanted to tell Bradley he was Harry Houdini, the one who had originated the act. Instead, he offered, "We can make anything come out of the trunk."

"Not interested. What else you got?"

Ehrich looked to Tesla, who shrugged. Behind the trunk, Amina raised her head and stared blankly.

Bradley shifted in his seat, preparing to get up. "Well, if that's all you got, I can grab some lunch before the afternoon shift shows up."

Ehrich glanced around the props laid out for the next performance and noticed the Lunatic's straitjacket. The hint of an idea tickled the back of his brain.

"Mr. Shaw, what if I told you I have an act that could pack this tent for the rest of the summer? And all I have to do is put my life in mortal danger."

Bradley stopped and turned. "The chance of death? How big?"

"Huge."

"Now you have my interest. What's the stunt?"

Ehrich motioned to the straitjacket. "I would have to use this. Do you mind?"

"The straitjacket? Sure. What do you need it for?"

"It's better if I show you."

Bradley waved the go-ahead.

Ehrich motioned Amina and Tesla to join him. He instructed them: "Truss me up tight and make it look good."

Amina nodded. Tesla grabbed the jacket. Ehrich placed his arms inside the long sleeves and turned around. Amina strapped the buckles that lined the back. He crossed his arms over his chest and let her fasten the straps, but he puffed out his chest and arms so he could create some slack when it came time to escape. The stench of the jacket made Ehrich wince. "Imagine me escaping from what no asylum patient has ever escaped from."

Amina cinched the final strap between Ehrich's legs. He gasped in pain and writhed in the jacket to adjust his stance.

Shaw shook his head. "Escape acts are boring. All they ever do is stand behind a curtain and grunt and groan while the audiences wait."

"Who said I was going to stand behind a curtain?"

Shaw fell silent.

Amina cleared the stage while Ehrich stepped to the front. Ba Tian's soldiers had trussed him up in a similar restraint on the *Oriental Clipper*, and he was able to free himself then. He was certain he could repeat the act. He thrashed himself from side to side as he struggled to loosen the straps of the canvas jacket. He bobbed up and down, trying to shake the straps off. He growled in pain and, slowly but surely, he was able to work his arms loose. Bradley leaned forward. Ehrich squirmed his right arm out of the straitjacket's collar. He reached behind his neck and unfastened the top strap. Then he howled as he tried to shake the jacket open.

"I think I've dislocated my shoulder," Ehrich panted.

"Do you want to stop?" Amina asked.

"No, no. I'll keep going."

He worked his hand through the bottom of the jacket and loosened the strap between his legs. Then, after several minutes of writhing, he peeled the jacket off as if he were taking off a snug sweater. He threw the canvas jacket to the stage.

Bradley clapped. "Impressive! I like it, but I thought you said your life might be in danger."

Ehrich smiled. "Yes, it will be when you hang me upside down from the top of your tent."

The rail-thin man gasped. "Are you serious?"

"The higher I can hang, the better the optics. We can wrap me up in chains and ropes as well. The more shackles, the higher the danger. One slip and I'll fall to my death. Once people catch wind of this act, they'll beg for more, and they'll flock to your tent."

"You're counting on the morbid curiosity of a bunch of suckers."

"Tell you what, Mr. Shaw. Give us a week. We'll take a cut of the gate. We don't sell, you don't pay."

Bradley scratched the side of his crooked nose. "What's the catch?"

"You pay for the handbills so we can promote the act."

He shook his head. "That's money out of my pocket. I pay for the handbills, but I take back the costs from what you earn."

Ehrich sighed. "Sure. It's a deal."

"I'll start you next week."

"You won't be disappointed."

Amina's eyes widened, but she said nothing until Bradley walked out of the tent. "What do you think you're doing? We're using our act as a cover. Now you're stepping into the public eye? It's like you want the hunters to catch us."

"Trust me, Amina. Trust me."

—⌁—

Two days later, Ehrich revealed his plan. He needed to learn about the execution schedule and only the hunters would know. They weren't likely to reveal this information, but they might have some paperwork in the station house. The trick was to slip inside.

With flyers in hand, Ehrich sauntered through the Coney Island crowd. People barely paid attention to him as he tried to promote the show. The best way to be invisible was to try to sell people something. As soon as the vacationers saw the handbills, they glanced away. Even the hunters ignored him.

Amina, Tesla, and Dash lingered on the fringe of the crowd to enjoy Ehrich's futile attempts to attract attention. He gave up handing out the flyers and stuffed them into the back of his pants.

"Gather round one and all," he announced. "I am Hardeen the Handcuff King. There is no shackle or rope that can hold me for long. Tie me up and I will shed the bonds as easily as a gentleman doffs his hat for a lady."

Tesla leaned to Amina and Dash. "Do you think we should help?"

Amina shook her head. "Some people are starting to take notice."

The crowd turned their attention to Ehrich. Even a trio of hunters seemed amused. He pointed a finger at the stocky hunter in the middle. "In fact, you could even lock me up in a Demon Watch jail, and I'd be free before you could blink."

The crowd laughed.

"Ah, I see you don't believe me," Ehrich said. "Well, there is only one way to find out and that is for the hunters to lock me up. That is if they can catch me."

The stocky one responded. "Stop wasting our time and get on your way. Sell your show somewhere else."

"I don't think you heard me the first time, sir. I said, if you can even catch me. Perhaps you can't hear because something's blocking your ear." Ehrich reached up to the man's ear and plucked a coin. "Well, what do you know? Hunters do have 'sense.'"

The crowd roared. More people inched forward to catch the banter. The stocky hunter and his two companions were not amused.

"Get on your way," he growled.

"Let's turn it over to the people. Do you want to see a great escape? Or do you want to watch hunters idly standing in front of a half-finished stage?"

Amina shouted from the back. "Lock him up."

Others in the crowd joined in until a chant began. Like the conductor of an orchestra, Ehrich led the crowd, urging louder voices.

The stocky hunter had had enough. He grabbed Ehrich by the back of the collar. "Okay, bright stuff. You wanted to be locked up? I'm happy to oblige." He barked at the others. "Jenson, stay here. Derrick, keep the crowd back. This loudmouth is going to learn some manners."

"Sure thing, Walter," Jenson answered.

Derrick tried to hold the crowd back as Walter escorted Ehrich away from the execution site, but he was swept up among the masses eager to see what Ehrich was going to do.

Tesla turned to Amina. "Should we help?"

"You go. Keep an eye on him. Dash and I will watch the site."

The lanky scientist joined the throng of people. The Demon Watch station was a few blocks away. Walter hauled Ehrich up the steps to the building while Derrick, out of breath, caught up and tried to hold back the people.

"Back off, everyone. This is Demon Watch business."

Ehrich turned and waved to the crowd. "Stay here. I'll be out shortly. No prison can hold the great Hardeen, the Handcuff King."

"I wouldn't bet on it," Walter said as he shoved Ehrich inside.

At a desk, a female hunter worked on paperwork. "What's this?" she asked.

"Some yahoo trying to make a name for himself. He was disrupting the site. Thought it might be good for him to cool his heels in the cell for a few hours."

She fished the keys from her pocket. They jangled in her hand as she strolled to the cell at the back of the room and opened the metal door. It swung open and she stepped aside. Walter shoved Ehrich into the cell and followed him in. He pressed Ehrich against the wall and patted him down, taking away the handbills and emptying his pockets.

"This is the most excitement I've had all week," she said. "What's your beef with him?"

"Claims no prison can hold him."

"It's true. As soon as you leave, I will happily spring myself free from the cell. Then you can catch the rest of my act at the big circus tent at the end of the boardwalk."

The female hunter chuckled. "The things you performers will do for attention."

Ehrich flashed a smile. "If I can't escape from this cell within the next half-hour, you two will get free tickets to my show."

Walter folded his arms over his chest. "If you can't escape, there won't be a show."

"There's always a sceptic in the crowd." Ehrich turned to the female hunter. "You believe me, don't you?"

She shrugged. "I'm just bored and looking for a distraction from my paperwork."

"Leave me in the cell for half an hour. I guarantee I will be out before you come back."

"A dollar says he'll still be here," the stocky hunter said.

She beamed. "Two."

"All right then. I'll pay each of you five dollars if I'm still locked in this cell when you return, but I warn you. Hardeen, the Handcuff King has never failed."

"Until now," the female hunter said. She approached Ehrich and slapped a pair of Darby shackles on his wrists. The thick cold metal bit into Ehrich's wrists as the hunter screwed in the key. Then she stepped out of the cell and slammed the door shut.

"You're not going anywhere, Hardeen," said Walter.

"Except to get our money," the female hunter quipped. They laughed and left.

—◦—\/\/\—◦—

Alone, Ehrich worked quickly. First, the shackles. He slammed the cuffs against the wall. His arms vibrated from the shock. He tried again and the shackles popped open and clattered to the stone floor. Ehrich kicked them to one side. As a hunter, he had played with the Darby shackles enough times to figure out their only weakness was a sharp blow to the right spot, and months of practice had helped him find the right spot.

Now, the cell door. He reached down to the sole of his shoe and popped the secret compartment on the heel to reveal his lock-pick set. He retrieved a hook pick and tension wrench then knelt at the cell door. He reached through the bars and around to the lock, inserting the prongs of the tension wrench into the keyhole. He worked the hook pick in from the other side and carefully lifted the pins holding the lock mechanism in place. In total, there should be four pins he'd have to lift. He listened for the distinct sound of a click when the pin had shifted into the right position. Within a few minutes, the door swung open. Ehrich hid his tools back in the heel of his shoe and rushed to the desk.

He didn't know what he might find, but he hoped there would be some paperwork concerning the execution plans. He glanced at the door. Outside, the crowds shouted encouragement for Ehrich to break out. He smiled and focused on the scattered sheets across the desk.

He rummaged through handwritten reports and schedules. He wasn't sure how much time had passed, but he had to hurry before the eager hunters returned to collect their cash. Then he spotted a piece of paper underneath the pile: a memo from Thomas Edison. He skimmed the missive and noted one line:

"Test of electrocution equipment with Topsy the Elephant."

Ehrich sucked in air. Edison planned to test the equipment on the elephant. He read further. The test was set for a week from today. A successful test would mean the execution would follow within a day or two, depending on how long it would take to transport the prisoners to Coney Island.

A rattle at the door. Someone was opening it. Ehrich had to move quickly. He slipped the note under the pile then flopped into the chair and kicked his feet up on top of the desk.

The door opened and the two hunters gaped at the sight of their prisoner lounging at the desk. Behind them, a few of the more eager gawkers peered over the couple's shoulders.

"He's out! He's sitting at the desk. He did it!"

The crowd roared. The hunters stared at Ehrich, bewildered. He lowered his feet and sauntered out to take in the adoration of the crowd.

"There is more to see at the big circus tent. My show starts Monday. Hardeen, the Handcuff King. Don't forget the name."

The people cheered. Ehrich basked in the glory and took a bow.

TROUBLE IN PURGATORY

In the performers village behind the main tent, Ehrich informed his friends about his discovery in the Demon Watch jail, which triggered Tesla's anger. The lanky scientist began to pace back and forth in front of the bench the others sat on.

"Edison should never have been allowed near my generators. I knew I should have destroyed them before I left the island. I intend to remedy that now."

Amina pointed out. "We should wait, sir."

"Are you going to let the elephant die?" Dash asked.

Ehrich turned to his brother. "We'll figure out something before the demonstration."

"We should set it free."

"The demonstration needs to go ahead," Amina said. "To draw out Ba Tian's generals and soldiers."

"That's cruel," Dash said. "The elephant never did anything to anyone."

Ehrich shook his head. "I agree with Mr. Tesla. We have to take out the generators now."

Amina stood up from the bench. "I know you're all worried about what's going to happen, but our plan was to discredit Edison. If we sabotage the equipment before he has a chance to test it in front of the public, he'll try again. We have to time this perfectly or else all will fail. The actual execution is sure to draw a larger crowd. The more eyes, the less credibility he'll have."

"We can accomplish the same thing at the demonstration," Ehrich argued.

Dash grabbed Ehrich's arm. "We can't let the animal die. She did nothing."

Tesla waved his hand. "I'll need to get near the generators to render the coils ineffective."

"The technicians should be able to fix that," Amina pointed out. "We're going to need something bigger."

Tesla considered this for a moment, drumming his fingers against his cheek. Finally, he agreed. "I could manufacture a device that I can plant on the generators and direct their energy inward to cause an implosion. I'll need time to do that. I don't know if I'll have it ready in time for the demonstration."

"Then it's settled. We wait until the execution."

The Weisz brothers began to protest. Amina shut them up with a stern glare.

"We wait."

The lanky scientist agreed. "I won't need more than a minute or two at the generator to affix the device. I had better secure the materials I need for this."

Amina nodded. "In the meantime, I think we should scout the site and find the best way to get Mr. Tesla near the generators."

Dash disagreed. "We have to save the elephant."

Ehrich patted his brother's leg. He sounded so earnest and sincere. How on Earth could he be the assassin?

—⁓⁓—

Tesla rummaged in his rucksack and fished out two small devices. He passed one to Amina. "Take this."

She turned over the black box, examining the strange circle with dots on the face of the box and the silver toggle on the side.

"Is it a weapon?"

Mr. Tesla extended an antenna from the top of his device and signalled Amina to do the same with hers. "Better. I call them communicators. Toggle the switch and speak into the circle. Your voice will be turned into radio signals and broadcast to the other device. We'll be able to stay in contact with each other."

She flipped the silver toggle and spoke into the device. "Testing."

Her voice squawked out of the device in Tesla's hands.

Ehrich and Dash rushed over. "Amazing," the Weisz brothers said in unison.

Tesla smiled. "It's a variation of the remote control for the submarine. At some point, I imagine the entire world connected wirelessly. We might be able to talk to someone in Australia all the way from New York."

Ehrich took the device and toggled the switch. He spoke into the circle, but his voice did not sound out of Amina's communicator.

Tesla pointed at the toggle on Amina's device. "Once you've sent your message, toggle the switch to the other position to listen. Always remember to switch over or else the communicator will not be able to receive."

She let go of the toggle and Ehrich tried again. Now his voice blasted out of the other communicator.

Amina beamed. "You should have left one with Mr. Serenity so we could update him."

Tesla shook his head. "Unfortunately, the range of the devices is limited. The signal is good for about a mile or so. Less if the radio waves have to travel through buildings, and I don't believe the signal can travel underground. At least, I haven't ascertained how."

Amina nodded. "Too bad. I'm hoping Mr. Serenity is making progress with the Infinity Coil."

"If I know my friend, he's already unlocked its secrets."

—·\/\/\—·

Mr. Serenity wasn't even close to success. In his lab, the rotund scientist angled the radiographometer to examine the Infinity Coil. The images on the screen were too numerous to count. He adjusted the dials to bring the images into focus, but more and more faces kept appearing.

He leaned closer, using a metal probe to tap the screen as he examined the myriad of faces. They seemed to shift, almost as if they were jockeying for positions at the front. He sighed and stepped back. Rubbing his eyes, he muttered, "There has to be an easier way."

He headed to the corner of the lab and rummaged through a wooden chest. He fished out a jade tael, the one Ning Shu had used as her weapon. Ehrich had recovered the tael from her lifeless body as a memento, and Mr. Serenity became the caretaker of this device, along with so many other artefacts of fallen comrades.

The green circle twisted on the leather strap dangling from Mr. Serenity's fingers. He eyed the smooth jade surface and the square hole in the centre. "Ning Shu, I hope you have a sentimental attachment to this," he muttered.

He dangled the jade tael near the mounted medallion and waited for its owner to heed its call.

The faces on the screen shifted, almost seeming to part. Mr. Serenity leaned closer. A tiny blip on the screen began to coalesce and take shape, slowly growing larger. He moved the tael closer to the screen and the blip moved toward it. The dance between the tael and the blip mesmerized the scientist. For a moment, he thought he smelled something burning. He glanced around the lab. Nothing was on fire, but the stench of sulphur was unmistakable.

He directed his attention back to the screen. The blip was taking on a clearer shape. A face was coming into focus. The other faces cleared away. Mr. Serenity smiled. He leaned closer. The features sharpened into two black eyes, an elegant nose and a thin-lipped smile with a pencil-thin moustache over the upper lip. Too late, Mr. Serenity realized he wasn't staring at the face of Ning Shu but that of a man.

He stepped back. The smell of sulphur filled the room. His eyes widened as black smoke poured out of the Infinity Coil. The wisps of smoke curled toward Mr. Serenity. He opened his mouth to scream.

THE SPY

The hot day attracted many New Yorkers to Coney Island. Couples and families strolled up and down the boardwalk. People frolicked in the ocean while families watched from the beach. A few stalwart men swam past the safety markers to impress their dates. Crowds lingered near the demonstration site, gawking at the generators. Amid the tourists, Ehrich and Dash hawked their flyers.

"You will see a man risk his life," Ehrich proclaimed. "It may be my last ever performance. Come and see the Great Hardeen escape from a straitjacket while hanging upside down from the top of a circus tent."

A few tourists grabbed flyers. The rest were more interested in the work at the execution site. The technicians laid out cable while a supervisor watched over them, directing workers to secure connections into the generators. The hunters kept the gawkers at bay. The shackled elephant mournfully trumpeted the proceedings every now and then, punctuating the surreal scene.

A tourist guide waved a hand at the elephant in chains near the stage. "That's Topsy. Rumours have it that she was the last elephant P.T. Barnum used in his act before he shut down the Greatest Show on Earth. Others say she was just a flea-ridden beast that hopped from one cheap circus to another until she landed at Sea Lion Park right here on Coney Island."

"Is she too old to perform? Are they putting her down because she's past her prime?" a woman asked.

"No, she's got a temper," the guide said. "One of the trainers was trying to control her with a prod. She didn't take a liking to it, so she swatted him with her trunk. He kept it up and, well, she decided to turn his head into a squashed melon."

Dash shook his head. "An elephant wouldn't have done it unless she was provoked."

The guide ignored Dash. "Rumour has it Thomas Edison paid a dollar for the right to execute her, and the owner said it was the best offer he was ever going to get for the animal."

"She didn't know any better. She was defending herself," Dash pleaded.

"Kid, her fate's sealed either way."

Dash was about to argue, but Ehrich grabbed his brother's arm. "Let's keep working."

The boy reluctantly followed his big brother.

The Weisz brothers skirted the crowd, wide enough to keep an eye on the execution site. Ehrich slowed when he reached the backside of the site. A scruffy technician worked near the back of the transformer. He glanced around nervously as he tried to figure out which cable to pick up. He settled on a thick one and snaked it away from the transformer.

"He has no idea what he's doing," Ehrich muttered.

"What *is* he doing?" Dash asked.

"I'm not sure, but he looks out of place as a technician. Let's keep an eye on him."

The scruffy technician reached into his pocket for something. He glanced around and noticed Ehrich watching him. He put the item back in his pocket and backed away from the generator.

Ehrich pulled Dash along the cordon to find a better view. The man veered around the elephant and headed away from the worksite. He left the crowds and made his way to a row of establishments near the train station. A combination of shops and taverns lined the street. The scruffy man entered one of the pubs.

Ehrich was torn. He could go in, but with Dash in tow they would arouse suspicion. He didn't want to leave his brother alone. He reached into his pocket and pulled out the communication device. He toggled the switch and spoke into the device. "Mr. Tesla, I've followed a suspicious-looking man to a pub near the train station. Come to us quickly. I'll keep watch out here to make sure he doesn't leave, but I think someone should go inside."

He waited. No response.

Dash nudged him. "Switch off the toggle."

Ehrich did and Tesla's voice answered from the device. "... on ... our ... way."

He pocketed the device and sat beside his brother.

"You can go in, Ehrich. I can keep an eye out for Mr. Tesla and Amina."

"Thanks for the offer, Dash, but I think it's better if we're all together. We don't want anything to happen to the group."

"You mean you don't trust me."

Ehrich skirted the truth. "No, it took me so long to find you, I'm not about to lose you again. Mother would kill me."

"If we ever get back home," Dash pointed out.

"Don't worry. We will."

"What do you think this guy has to do with anything?" Dash asked.

"I've trained as a hunter," Ehrich explained. "And after a certain number of patrols, you learn that the people who have something to hide, or some kind of agenda, act a certain way. He kept looking around, as if he was worried someone might catch on to him. That kind of behaviour is something that makes him stand out."

"He's a spy?"

"Quite possibly."

"I'll go in," Dash offered. "I'll pretend that I'm lost or something. You can slip in while everyone's watching me. They won't know we're together."

Ehrich considered the offer. One way or another, he couldn't leave Dash alone. In the pub, at least, he could keep an eye on him in case he tried to send a message to someone.

"Well?" Dash asked.

Ehrich dusted off his jacket. "You go first. I'll come after you've had a chance to settle in."

Dash headed to the pub. Over the door, the pub sign read: "Robber's Roost." Ehrich decided not to leave Dash alone for long. He jogged into the pub right after his brother.

•—◦◦◦—•

The exterior wall appeared to have seen better days, being soiled with either spilled ale or urine. The mix of ruffians, both male and female, ignored Ehrich. Instead, they eyed Dash with the same kind of hunter instinct as a cougar about to maul its prey.

"You don't belong here, kid," a man with an eyepatch growled.

Dash launched into his act.

"I can't find my mom or dad. I'm lost. Are they here?" Dash raised the register of his voice to sound pathetic and helpless.

"Well, if they're here, they're probably dead," the man joked.

The others laughed. Ehrich found a table at the edge of the pub and scanned the room for the scruffy man. He spotted him at the other end of the pub, sitting at a table by himself. Relieved that his brother wasn't going to run or contact the scruffy man, Ehrich sat back and watched Dash in action.

His brother began to rub his eyes and pretend to cry. The laughter stopped as a barmaid rushed to Dash and wiped his face with the hem of her skirt. She scolded the others. "Brutes. Can't you see the boy is afraid? Are you hungry?"

Dash's lip quivered. "No. Not really. Maybe."

The man with the eyepatch muttered, "He's probably fishing for a free meal."

The barmaid escorted Dash to the counter while the patrons returned to their carousing. No one noticed Ehrich at all. He smiled at Dash's ingenuity. He had employed misdirection to perfection, allowing Ehrich to slip into the pub unnoticed. Another barmaid approached him.

"I'll take an ale," Ehrich said.

The brusque woman with tattoos up and down her massive arms threw a towel over her shoulder and leaned against the table. "I haven't seen you here before."

"But I'm sure you're familiar with my good friends," Ehrich said. He slapped a fistful of coins on the table.

Her eyes widened at the sight. "One ale coming up, sir."

Ehrich checked on Dash, winning over another barmaid at the counter. He had his charms, Ehrich had to give him that. He returned his attention to the job at hand.

A man in a long black duster limped toward the scruffy man's table. The source of the limp was the man's peg leg, a wooden stump where his left leg should have been. Ehrich couldn't shake the feeling that something was familiar about this man. He had to see the man's face.

The barmaid slammed a mug of ale on the table and scooped up the coins. He nodded at her, grabbed his mug, and sauntered to the bar where the barmaids were cooing over Dash. He leaned closer to hear.

"What did you find out?" the man with the wooden leg asked.

"Edison's boys are getting mighty close to finishing. We might need to slow them down a hair or two," the scruffy technician said with a southern drawl.

"Whatever it takes, Hobbs. Do you hear me?"

"Yes, Captain Farrier. Whatever it takes."

Ehrich froze. Farrier. The man with the wooden leg was the former commander of the hunters. He had betrayed everyone on Devil's Island by making a deal with Ba Tian to enable him to invade the island.

The last Ehrich had seen of Farrier was in the battle on Devil's Island where Farrier had allowed Ba Tian and his exoskeletons to slip past the defences. Farrier planned to let Ba Tian gain control of the Demon Gate portal and bring over his invading army. If it hadn't been for Amina and Mr. Serenity, the warlord would now have the means to invade New York. In the melee, the traitor Farrier had fled the fight. Ehrich had assumed the man had crawled under a rock never to be seen again. He was wrong. Questions reeled through his mind. Why was the former Demon Watch commander here? What was his end goal? Why was he spying on the execution site? Ehrich moved closer to listen.

Farrier turned at the same time, revealing his battle-scarred face and menacing eyes. Ehrich tried to slip away, but Farrier's eyes widened with recognition. "Weisz," he hissed.

THE CHASE

Farrier stood up, resting his hand against the chair. "You," he hissed. "He's one of them," he said to the scruffy technician.

Two against one. Ehrich backed away.

"Spy!" Farrier yelled.

The patrons spun around.

Ehrich angled his body so he could keep an eye on Farrier and defend himself from the ruffians now rising from their seats.

"Back off," Ehrich said. "This is Demon Watch business. That man's a traitor to Demon Watch."

The man with the eyepatch growled. "I hate coppers. Always sticking their noses where they don't belong."

Farrier roared, "Ten dollars to the man who teaches this mutt some manners."

This was all the encouragement they needed. The ruffians advanced on Ehrich while Farrier and Hobbs headed to the exit.

Ehrich wanted to tackle Farrier, but he had to run the gauntlet of thugs. He dropped the mug on the ground and grabbed a chair to defend himself.

"You don't think I'm here on my own, do you?" Ehrich asked. "I have reinforcements outside. One whistle and you're all going to be in Darby shackles by the end of the day."

"He's bluffing," the man with the eyepatch said.

But the others were not so sure. A few backed away. Two advanced on Ehrich. He raised the chair, ready to fight.

Suddenly Dash screamed, "Fire!"

Everyone turned. Flames ran along the bar counter. The barmaids rushed to put out the fire. A few patrons joined in to help. Farrier turned around and urged the others, "Grab the kid. Don't let him get out!"

No one was sure what to do. Ehrich used this momentary distraction to act. He hurled the chair at the man with the patch, then flipped over a table at a group of ruffians coming at his flank. "Dash! Go!"

A ruffian tried to grab Ehrich. He slammed into the thug's chest and shoved him against the wall. Ehrich glanced back. Farrier and Hobbs helped the fallen man. Dash was stuck in the crowd of bar patrons. Ehrich had to lead the ruffians away. He bolted out of the pub.

Outside, Ehrich spotted Tesla and Amina. He veered toward them with four people on his heels. As he passed his friends he yelled, "Dash! He's inside."

Amina headed for the pub while Tesla joined Ehrich, leading the four men toward the beach. Ehrich outpaced the older man and had to loop back to encourage Tesla to pick up the pace. Each time he slowed, the thugs gained ground. Ehrich knew he'd have to confront them, but the odds were two to one in the thugs' favour. He needed an advantage.

Ehrich settled on a large beach umbrella propped in the sand. He veered toward it and snatched it out of the ground, upsetting the two teenagers kissing under it.

"Head for the pier, Mr. Tesla!" he shouted. "I'll slow them down."

The lanky scientist huffed and puffed through the sand while Ehrich charged the ruffians with the closed umbrella. He popped the umbrella open, hiding behind it. The thugs slowed, splitting off two to each side of the umbrella. Ehrich waited until he saw their shadows on the beach then dug the open umbrella into the sand and swung it up and to the left. He blinded one thug with sand and sent the other one back a few feet. He closed the umbrella and swung it at the remaining two thugs. The umbrella cracked in half against a skull, sending the ruffian to the sand. He did not rise.

Ehrich speared the other thug. The force of the collision knocked the wind out of his lungs and he collapsed on the ground, gasping for air. Ehrich drove his knee into the man's chin and knocked him out.

He glanced at the two conscious thugs. One was wiping the sand out of his eyes while the other recovered. It was the man with the eyepatch. He pulled a large cleaver from his belt and slashed the air. Ehrich backed away, holding up what was left of the umbrella to defend himself.

The man with the eyepatch chopped at the wooden pole, closing in on his foe. Ehrich backpedalled. The other thug rose up and flanked Ehrich. He was outmanned.

Then out of the corner of his eye, he caught a glimpse of a figure charging fast toward the two of them. Tesla! The scientist flung something up into the air and a spider web flashed in the sunlight. A fishing net landed over the thug. Tesla slammed into the trapped man and knocked him to the sand. The man with the patch gaped at the scene, giving Ehrich an opening. He swung the remains of the pole across the man's nose. Crack! the thug dropped his cleaver and fell to the sand, clutching his broken nose. Ehrich picked up the cleaver and waved it at his lone opponent. The man with the patch fled the scene.

"Good work," Tesla said, clapping his hand on the boy's back.

"I saw Farrier in the pub," Ehrich said, trying to gulp in air. "The spy is working for him. I'm not sure why, but he must still be working for Ba Tian's army."

"We must alert Amina. Your communicator. Quick."

Ehrich handed his mentor the device. Tesla clicked on the button. "Amina, do you hear me? Hello. Hello. Ahoy."

No response.

He tried again and again, but the device remained silent.

"Perhaps they are out of range," Tesla suggested, chewing his bottom lip.

•─wŵw─•

Hours later, Ehrich and Tesla found Amina and Dash back at the performers village. They looked none the worse for wear.

"Where were you two? We've been trying to get a hold of you."

Amina motioned Ehrich to sit down. "We tried to track the people who came out of the bar, but there were too many of them."

"Did you see Farrier?" Ehrich asked.

She shook her head. "The one who betrayed Demon Watch?"

"Yes. The spy was meeting with him."

"Why would Farrier be interested in the execution?" she asked.

"Who is this Farrier?" Dash asked.

Ehrich explained, "He used to be in charge of the Demon Watch. He oversaw the hunters, but he made a pact with Ba Tian. He was going to give the warlord access to the Demon Gate portal.

"Why would he side with a Dimensional?"

Amina answered Dash. "Because of what Ba Tian offered in exchange. The exoskeletons."

Tesla added, "Farrier believed the south should have won the Civil War. With the exoskeletons, he could remedy that problem. He had a few sympathetic southerners on his side."

Amina stiffened. "If Farrier's watching the site, that must mean his deal with Ba Tian is still on, and that means there are some generals still at large."

Ehrich agreed. "Farrier might be trying to rescue the rest of the generals so they can secure him the exoskeletons."

Tesla stroked his chin. "Possible. Now we must exercise even more caution. Enemies abound."

"He was talking to the spy at the execution site," Ehrich said. "Something big is going to happen."

"They're going to rescue the generals," Amina said. "But they can't do anything until the generals are at the execution site. That's when Farrier will strike."

Ehrich agreed. "We're going to have to keep a close watch on the site. Make sure we're ready for whatever Farrier has planned."

—◦WW◦—

Over the next few days, Amina, Dash, and Ehrich took shifts staking out the execution site while Tesla worked on the sabotage device. Amina kept Dash close, under the pretence that he had seen the spy and she had not, but she had another agenda, which was to keep an eye on Dash.

On the afternoon of the third day, the supervisor ran a test of the generators. They whirred to life and sparks flew from the donut-shaped heads at the top of the towers. The elephant trumpeted in panic while the appreciative crowd applauded at the mini-fireworks display. Time was running out with no sign of the spy or Farrier.

—◦-√√√-◦—

Later that afternoon, a larger crowd than usual had gathered around the generators and stage. Thomas Edison, the Demon Watch Commissioner, stood on stage, surrounded by reporters at the front of the platform.

"The equipment is test ready. We will demonstrate tomorrow with Topsy. She will be the largest creature ever to be electrocuted by alternating current electricity."

Tesla lurched forward, forcing Amina to restrain him.

"Sir, we'll have our chance to sabotage Edison's plans at the execution. We have to let him think this is working."

Tesla relented. "My apologies. My sense of justice tends to boil over when my reputation is on the line. I must redouble my efforts to complete the device."

"Can't we do something about it now?" Dash asked.

Ehrich patted the boy's shoulder. "Sorry. We have to wait."

"But the elephant."

Tesla shook his head. "I'm afraid even if I wanted to do something, I wouldn't have the device ready by the morning."

Ehrich glanced once more at the stage where Edison lapped up the attention. Tomorrow promised to be an interesting day.

CONEY ISLAND CHAOS

The next morning, word about the execution had spread quickly. When Ehrich's group arrived, nearly 300 people had gathered in front of the stage and watched the technicians prepare last-minute checks of the Tesla electrical towers.

Amina and Tesla veered off to one side of the crowd, angling toward the generators, while Ehrich and Dash headed closer to the side with the elephant. Hunters circulated around the giant beast as a technician hauled the cables to the shackled creature. Ehrich shuddered at the fate that would soon befall the animal. No one should ever have to suffer like this. He wondered if there was anything they might do to stop it, but he knew that any action might jeopardize their plan to flush out Farrier and his southerners. The elephant would have to be sacrificed for the greater good. Too bad the elephant didn't have a choice in the matter.

Ehrich scanned the crowd behind him, looking for any sign

of the scruffy man. Mostly, he saw gawking tourists, eager for the death about to unfold before them. Men and women alike seemed keen to witness the death of an animal. Ehrich had no idea what their fascination was. Perhaps it was the novelty of an execution with electricity. Maybe they were curious about death. Either way, they were drawn to this site in the same way his promise of risking his own life in the escape act brought people to the tent. People were morbid.

On the demonstration stage, Thomas Edison in a wool jacket wiped his brow. Though it was early morning, the man seemed to be sweating. Ehrich guessed that it wasn't from the heat but the fear of potential failure. He directed the technicians, barking orders at them to check every contact point. Taking the stage, the dignitaries began to arrive. They were not high-profile officials like the mayor or the governor. They were lower level officials, most likely sent here to observe and report their findings to their bosses. If the experiment worked, they would tell their superiors to attend the execution. If it failed, they would tell their bosses to lay the blame at Edison's feet. No wonder the man was sweating.

A few hunters lined up at the cordon, keeping the curious onlookers at bay. By the generators, there was the hum of activity as the technicians worked on the connections and the generators. Behind, more tourists gathered for the grisly demonstration.

"Stay close, Dash," Ehrich said. He glanced to the side where his brother was supposed to be. He was gone.

Ehrich searched the crowd for any sign of the boy. He called out for him as he pushed through the crowd surging forward. His worst fear hit Ehrich square in the gut. Dash was Kifo and using this as a means to slip away. He had to find the boy and fast. He pushed a grumpy onlooker out of the way.

"Dash!" he called out.

No answer. He looked around, helpless and panicking.

—W—

By the generators, Tesla vibrated with a different kind of panic. He wanted to leap over the cordon and rip the cables out of his beautiful generators. The towers were not built for this abomination of a display. With Edison touting the dangers of alternating current electricity coupled with the demonstration, there would be no way that people would dare to use Tesla's technology. His reputation would be shredded with one flip of a switch.

Amina grabbed his arm. "Easy, sir. Not yet."

Tesla nodded. "I must put an end to all of this."

"I understand, but the risk is too great."

He tried to pull away from her, but they both stopped when they heard Ehrich's voice over the crowd.

"Dash!"

Amina strained to see over the crowd. She couldn't see her companion but she was sure she heard his voice.

"Something's wrong, Mr. Tesla." She pushed through the crowd in the direction of Ehrich's last position. The lanky scientist followed.

They pushed through the crowd until they found Ehrich at the far edge. Amina asked, "Where's your brother?"

"I don't know. He slipped away. We have to find him."

Tesla shook his head. "The demonstration is about to begin. We have to stop it."

"If Kifo has possessed Dash, we have bigger problems," Ehrich said.

"Are you sure he's not just lost?" Amina asked.

"I don't know. That's why we have to find him."

The loud trumpet of Topsy the Elephant distracted them. At first, Ehrich believed the elephant was afraid of the crowds. Then when the people began screaming, he knew something else was at play. People scattered from the site as the angry elephant charged ahead, knocking hunters to the ground and trampling on the fallen.

Amina pulled at Ehrich's arm. "The elephant is on the rampage. Run!"

Topsy knocked down a hunter. Another hunter fired her dynatron pistol into the creature's hide. Big mistake. The elephant reared up and came down hard on the hunter. The crowd shrieked in terror as the elephant now knocked over the cordon and charged at them. People fled in all directions.

Caught in the mob, Ehrich, Amina, and Tesla surged ahead to look for Dash. Amina and Tesla were swept back. Ehrich navigated through the crowd and came out the other side. On the beach, he spotted Dash running toward the pier.

Ehrich sprinted down the boardwalk after the boy, worried Kifo had possessed Dash again. He wished he had a weapon but all he had were his wits. He poured on the speed and caught up to his brother, grabbing him by the collar and yanking him back. He prepared for a fight but Dash only squirmed and yelled.

"Let go."

"Where do you think you're going?" Ehrich demanded.

The boy pointed down the beach. The scruffy man was jogging toward a boathouse.

"You were tracking the spy?" Ehrich asked. "You should have called for me."

"I didn't want to lose him. Once I knew where he was, I was going to come back to you."

Ehrich let go of his brother and pulled out his communicator. He toggled the switch on and spoke into the device. "Amina, Mr. Tesla. Do you hear me?"

He toggled off and waited a minute, keeping his eye on the scruffy man.

"I ... hear ... you," Mr. Tesla's voice sounded from the speaker.

"Head to the boathouse by the pier. We have found the spy."

"On our way."

Ehrich pocketed the communicator. He and Dash headed down the beach toward the boathouse. Two men in demon hunter uniforms welcomed the scruffy man as he drew near. He could just make out their southern accents. They were Farrier's soldiers in disguise. The traitor had to be near.

The spy entered the boathouse and Ehrich veered past it, pretending to be a wandering tourist. The hunters watched the two brothers. Ehrich didn't want to alert the people inside, so he continued to walk past the structure, leading Dash away, but his brother had another idea.

Dash stopped and turned toward the boathouse. "I want to see the boats!"

"What are you doing?" Ehrich hissed.

"You promised I could see the boats. I want to see them now!"

"Come with me."

Dash whispered. "You want to see who's in there, don't you?"

Now they had everyone's attention. Ehrich grabbed Dash's hand and tried to pull his brother away. The boathouse door opened and Farrier limped out. Ehrich had expected to see him, but not the man right behind him: Ole Lukoje.

The raggedy man's eyes widened with recognition. "Get them!" he yelled as he pushed past Farrier.

The hunters chased the boys under the pier with Ole Lukoje sprinting to catch up. Three against two. The odds weren't in Ehrich's favour. He scanned the wooden posts around them for any way to climb up, but it was either jump in the ocean or fight.

He pushed Dash behind a pillar and warned, "Stay put. Don't do anything until I tell you."

Again, Dash had his own ideas. He raised his hands and turned to the approaching hunters, who had their dynatron pistols trained on the boy. "Don't shoot. It's me."

"Dash! What are you doing?" Ehrich cried. "Get back behind the post."

He ignored Ehrich's orders. Instead, Dash advanced toward Ole Lukoje and his allies. Both warriors kept their weapons trained on the boy, ready to fire. "Tell them to lower their weapons. I'm no threat. I'm one of you. Don't you recognize me? I am Kifo."

Ehrich's heart sank. His suspicions were right. His brother was lost to him.

The raggedy man tilted his head to one side then rubbed his steel finger along his hooked nose. "Yes-s-s, but you chos-s-s-e a different body. Why did you return to the original one?"

"A situation arose that forced my hand. I don't think Ba Tian would take kindly to you hurting his biggest asset."

Ole Lukoje motioned the hunters to stand down. "Lower your weapons-s-s."

They obeyed and stopped. Ole Lukoje cut between the two of them and cocked his head to the side as he examined Dash.

"What happened to you? I thought you were apprehended along with the res-s-st of the generals-s-s on the airsh-sh-ship."

"I managed to hitch a ride in a body until we reached the rebels' hideout. Then I decided to choose a body that better suited my purposes. You still have to deal with Ehrich."

The hunters turned and aimed their pistols at Ehrich's position. He squeezed himself tight behind the pillar.

"I had hoped that you didn't perish-sh-sh on the airsh-sh-ship."

Dash spread his hands out. "I'm disappointed that you didn't come looking for me earlier. I had to spend time in their Purgatory until I found a way to the surface. Now we have the means to take down the entire rebel force in one swoop. First, we have to take care of this pest."

"I will dis-s-spatch him with pleas-s-s-ure."

The boy waved him off. "No. I should have the pleasure. Give me a weapon," he barked at the female hunter near him.

She hesitated, looking to Ole Lukoje for direction. The raggedy man smiled. "If he wants-s-s the opportunity, let him take it."

Ehrich searched for some kind of weapon. He was defenseless against the four intruders. He looked beyond the beach for any sign of Amina or Tesla. No. He was alone against the four.

The female hunter handed her dynatron pistol to Dash. He took the weapon and hefted it in his hand for a second. He cracked a smile at the male hunter, pointed at his chest and fired. The stunned man stiffened into convulsions, an electro-dart jutting out of his chest, and fell to the sand, twitching. Dash turned to the female hunter and fired into her stomach. She fell, trying to pull the dart from her abdomen.

Ole Lukoje sprang into action and tackled Dash to the ground before the boy could fire a third shot. Ole Lukoje hissed, "Clever boy."

Ehrich spun around the pillar and charged at the pair struggling on the sand.

"You will pay the ultimate pric-c-c-e." Ole Lukoje raised his metal claw high up to bring down on the boy's face.

Ehrich leapt across the sand and slammed his body into the raggedy man, knocking him to the ground. He grabbed the man's wrists and tried to pin him. Ole Lukoje was faster, twisting his body to one angle and squirming out from under Ehrich. He slashed backward, catching part of Ehrich's arm, ripping the fabric of his shirt to shreds and cutting into the flesh u..derneath. Ehrich grabbed his arm and backed away.

"You made a fatal error, coming here," Ole Lukoje said. "It will be your final mis-s-stake."

He advanced. Ehrich steeled himself for the attack, raising his arms in a defensive posture. Dash scrambled to grab the dynatron pistol in the sand.

The raggedy man smiled as he curled his metal fingers. "I will s-s-savour this-s-s moment."

He slashed. Ehrich blocked the blow with his arm, but he left his other side open for a second slash. Ehrich screamed in pain and grabbed his cheek. A fresh flow of blood oozed between his fingers. The raggedy man knocked the boy to the ground and perched on his chest ready to strike again.

"Stop," Dash said, holding the pistol in his shaking hands. "Get off my brother!"

Ole Lukoje looked up.

"Now!"

The raggedy man smiled. "I think we have you outnumbered, little one."

Dash turned around. A dozen armed hunters trained their weapons on Dash and Ehrich. In front of the hunters, Amina and Tesla knelt in the sand, their heads bowed. Behind them stood Ba Tian, the crimson warlord.

THE WARLORD RETURNS

"A lovely reunion, don't you agree, Ehrich?" Ba Tian asked. "Let go of Amina and Mr. Tesla."

"Tell your brother to drop his weapon."

Ehrich said nothing.

Ba Tian sighed. "I'm not in the habit of asking twice. Kill the girl and the old man if the boy still has the weapon in three seconds."

Dash slowly lowered the pistol to the ground and kicked it across the sand.

Ole Lukoje smiled as he scooped up the weapon. He wrapped his metal hand around the boy's soft neck. The tips of the talons pierced the skin slightly, drawing a trickle of blood.

"Let go of him," Ehrich ordered.

"This-s-s little mutt has more s-s-spirit than all of you combined. He is-s-s dangerous-s-s."

Dash struggled, kicking at the man as he gasped for air.

"I said let him go," Ehrich pleaded.

"I enjoy watching you s-s-suffer. For what you did to me, this-s-s is-s-s the perfect revenge."

"You kill us, you'll draw attention to your operation," Ehrich warned.

Ba Tian chuckled. "No, the hunters are still trying to capture that crazy elephant my associates freed. A perfect distraction, don't you agree? There is no way anyone would care about a few bodies that happen to wash up on the shore."

"Let Dash go. Take it out on me, Ole Lukoje."

"But I am taking it out on you. I will take away all that you hold dear. Firs-s-s-st, your brother. Then your companions-s-s. I will sh-sh-show you their beating hearts-s-s before I pulp them in my hand."

"No!" Ehrich screamed. He lunged, but the raggedy man was ready. He lifted Dash into the air.

"Come any clos-s-ser and the s-s-spray of your kin's-s-s blood will wash-sh-sh over your flims-s-sy dis-s-sguis-s-se."

Ehrich halted. "You know you want me and not anyone else. Let's finish it."

Behind the raggedy man, Ba Tian strode forward. "Enough! Put the boy down."

Ole Lukoje obeyed.

"What do you want from us?" Amina asked.

Ba Tian lumbered in front of her. "Before one starts a war, one must be careful to examine the wheels within the wheels. I believe you have a force amassed against me. I'd like to know where they are."

"They are somewhere you'll never find them."

Farrier limped over to the group and smiled. "Four people

here. I'm sure one of them will give up the rebels. All you need is the right pressure. I can provide that, Ba Tian."

The crimson warlord cracked a wicked smile.

Ehrich straightened up. "You want to know? I'll tell you. They are on your doorstep, ready to bring you down."

"I suspect if I remind them of what happened to their former worlds, they may have a change of heart," Ba Tian said. "And believe me, what I have planned will bring them back to the days of their worlds' destruction. Perhaps I shall visit your world as well."

Ehrich gritted his teeth and said nothing. He jammed his hands into his pockets. His right hand found the marbles that he had bought for Dash. He thought of their parents in Appleton, Wisconsin, and imagined his home destroyed by Ba Tian's exoskeletons. His hand clenched around the clay marbles as he gritted his teeth. He had to stop the warlord.

"Shall I begin with the boy?" Farrier asked.

Ehrich stood tall. "Ba Tian, if I tell you where to find the others, will you let my friends go?"

"He'll kill us all once he gets the information he needs," Amina pleaded.

"My word is my bond. I will not harm your friends."

"Show me a sign of good faith. Let Dash go."

"Ole Lukoje, do as he asks."

The raggedy man tilted his head to the side for a moment, then relented. Dash grabbed his neck to stop the trickle of blood and stumbled to Ehrich.

"Now I believe you had something to tell me."

Ehrich squeezed the marbles tighter in his hand until he felt them crumble in his pocket. He continued to squeeze.

"I'm waiting."

Ehrich withdrew his hand from his pocket. The marbles had been ground into dust. He approached the giant crimson warlord.

"Well? What do you have to say?"

Ehrich mumbled a few words.

Ba Tian cocked his head to one side to hear. "Say that again."

Again, Ehrich mumbled.

"I can't hear you." Ba Tian stooped closer.

Ehrich exploded into action, hurling the clay dust into Ba Tian's eyes, blinding the warlord. "Dash! Run!"

His brother took off down the sand with Ehrich close behind. Electro-darts whizzed past them, striking the wooden posts of the pier. Ole Lukoje howled as he and three hunters were in hot pursuit. The brothers zigged and zagged until they reached the water and dove into the sea. The darts sizzled in the water as they swam away from the shore.

Back on the beach, Amina slammed her flat hand into Farrier's throat. He fell, gasping for air as she deftly disarmed him and fired into the back of the hunter in front of her. Tesla turned and tried to disarm the woman next to him, but she was stronger and pushed him down. He fell on the sand with her on top, which offered Amina the perfect target. She fired into the woman's back. The hunter went into a seizure as Tesla bucked her off him and climbed to his feet.

Ba Tian clutched his face, trying to scrub the dust out. Ole Lukoje and the other hunters stood at the shoreline. Amina grabbed Tesla by the hand and sprinted back to the circus tent.

She glanced back at the water. The hunters stood at the waterline, reluctant to jump in after her friends. Ehrich and Dash would be safe, she hoped. Once she hit the boardwalk,

Amina slowed down and blended in with curious onlookers watching hunters surround the elephant. They herded the creature away from the stage, zapping it with their weapons. The beast reared up and brought down its front legs on a man who had moved too close. The crowd let out a collective gasp of revulsion as the man perished before their eyes.

"Just kill it!" an onlooker yelled.

Shouts of agreement filled the air.

The hunters zapped the animal again with no effect. The elephant reared again. A shot rang out and the elephant staggered back. Three more shots rang out and the elephant collapsed on the ground.

Amina searched for the origin of the shot, finally seeing a tall man on stage beside Edison. He lowered his rifle. Edison grabbed the man's sleeve and yelled at him. The tall man shoved Edison back.

Amina caught a part of their heated exchange. "I was a fool to let you do this demonstration, Edison! I should have put down my elephant the minute she turned on my trainer. Anything is better than this."

"My hunters had everything under control."

"One of your men is dead because of all this nonsense. Who cares about the electrocution?"

On the stage, Edison noticed that the people around him were now watching. He let go of the circus owner and dusted off his jacket. He then approached the microphone and waved for attention. "We have everything under control. We may not see a demonstration with the elephant, but you will see the full power of the Tesla generators when we proceed with the execution of the Dimensionals."

"He will not get away with this," Tesla hissed.

"If Ba Tian is here, we have to prepare for an attack."

"Amina, give me a few moments near the generators. That's all I need."

"No time for that, sir."

Too late. Tesla had slipped away from the crowd and was making his way to the generators. Amina inched toward him, prepared to fight anyone who might see him, but all eyes were focused on Edison on the stage.

"I have full confidence that the generators will work as intended. They are a deadly and unsafe thing, best used for killing rather than to power your homes and businesses." Edison droned on, while the tall man with the rifle glared at him.

"You're seriously going through with this? After all this ruckus?"

Edison puffed up his chest. "Yes, the people need to see the Dimensionals punished."

"This rifle ought to do the trick if you give me enough bullets."

Amina glanced at the elephant, where the hunters were crowded round, trying to figure out how to move the dead beast. Tesla stood alone by the generators. He straightened up and jogged back, unnoticed by the crowd.

"Let's see Edison explain this away."

"What did you do?"

"Nothing dangerous. Unless they know what to do, this execution will go off with a fizzle."

"If you've had enough fun, sir, we have to assemble the travellers for battle. We have to go back to Purgatory and rally the rebels for the fight."

Tesla's smile vanished. "Yes. Of course. What about Ehrich and Dash?"

"Your device," Amina said. "Will it have the range to reach them?"

"Only one way to find out."

He pulled out the communication device and turned it on. "Ehrich. Do you hear me?" No response. He tried multiple times but only static answered him.

"Maybe they're still in the water," Amina suggested.

"I hope they haven't been captured."

—⟋⟍⟋⟍⟋⟍—

On the other end of Coney Island, Ehrich and Dash emerged from the water, soaking wet. The summer sun beat down on them and gave them some relief from the chilly Atlantic waters. Ehrich began to loosen his clothes to wring them out, keeping an eye out for Ole Lukoje and Ba Tian. They were not to be seen.

Dash trotted down the beach to a blanket and some shirts laid out by tourists who had gone for a swim. He returned with clothes for the two of them. The shirts were big on Dash, but Ehrich fit into the pants snuggly. He bundled the wet clothes so they could change back once they were dry.

As Ehrich bundled his jacket, he noticed a bulge in the pocket. He reached in and pulled out the communicator. It was damp and he wondered if it would still work. He turned it on. "Amina. Mr. Tesla. Do you hear me?"

He waited a moment. Then Tesla's voice answered. "Yes. Yes. We're all right. Where are you?"

Ehrich replied. "We're near the train station. We have no place to hide and we have no idea where Ba Tian and his forces are."

"You need to get out of there, Ehrich. We are thinking we need to leave Coney Island."

"I'll wait for you at the train station."

"No. It's too risky. If Ba Tian's hunters are near, they'll spot you."

Dash tugged on Ehrich's shirt. "What about the elephant? We have to save the elephant."

Ehrich nodded. "Did you hear that Mr. Tesla?"

"Yes. Tell Dash I'm sorry, but it's too late. They killed Topsy."

Dash's eyes widened. "No! Monsters!"

"She was on a rampage. They had no choice, Dash. Ehrich, get out while you can. We'll catch up."

"Are you sure?"

"Yes, we'll find you in the city. Amina says we need to rally the others. Meet us back in Purgatory."

"Are you sure you'll be able to get out, sir?"

"Don't worry. Amina is with me. She won't let anything happen to me."

Ehrich switched off the communication device and turned to his brother. "Okay, let's go."

They rushed up the stairs. Ehrich paid for their tickets with the money he had found in the new pants pocket. As the brothers boarded the train, he looked back at Coney Island.

The train rolled out of the station and he took a moment to sit back and relax. Beside him, Dash rubbed his hands, trying to warm them up.

"What you did back there, Dash, it was risky."

"I know, but if you thought I might have been this Kifo, I figured they might, too."

"Well. Next time warn me about what you're going to do."

Dash smiled. "I'm hoping there is no next time."

Ehrich punched his brother in the arm. "I'm going to make sure there isn't."

It felt good to joke around with his brother again. Though the threat of Ba Tian loomed over them, he savoured the moment when he could connect with his brother as they had done before any of this mess had started. He felt like he was home again, and he only hoped they'd be back to their real home soon.

A gasp from the passengers distracted him. Everyone on the train was looking out the window at the approaching city skyline. Plumes of smoke rose from various parts of the city. New York was on fire.

THE TUNNEL

Ehrich itched to get off the train as he looked out the window at the black plumes of smoke snaking up to the sky from various parts of Manhattan. He had no idea what had caused such widespread fires, but he feared this might have something to do with Ba Tian. He wondered if the warlord had been able to secure the exoskeletons and was now launching an attack on the city.

When the train finally arrived at the station, the two Weisz brothers joined the crowd streaming to the exit. They weren't the only ones interested in seeing where the fire was. Ehrich pushed through the crowd. Beside him, Dash clung to the back of Ehrich's jacket as they made their way off the platform and down the stairs to the street level. Ehrich eyed the nearest column of smoke and started toward it. It seemed to be coming from the Bowery area. He navigated the streets, which were now filled with spectators emerging from shops and offices to survey the smoke. No one paid attention to the two boys zigzagging through the crowds. Ehrich quickened his pace as he neared the black plume. As he reached the Bowery a few blocks later, a quiet sense of dread began to take hold of him. He recognized the streets and calculated the sources of the smoke.

"Dash, we have to run. Keep up."

"Wait. Wait! I'm coming."

Ehrich didn't look back. He sprinted the next three blocks until he reached a corner and turned to see black smoke engulfing a building that wasn't burning. The smoke was coming from the cellar doors leading to the basement. The guardian he had seen earlier when they had come to the surface stood among the others, watching helplessly. The fire was coming from under the ground. Purgatory.

Ehrich rushed to the woman and grabbed her arm. "What happened?"

Her eyes were moist with tears and her face covered with soot. At first she didn't recognize Ehrich, but he pulled her close and her eyes widened with recognition. "Thank goodness you left when you did."

"Don't worry about me. What happened here?"

"I don't know. One minute I was selling my wares; the next the ground shook. At first I thought it was a tremor but, a few minutes later, smoke began to pour out of the cellar doors. I tried to investigate. It looked like the smoke was coming from the pneumatic tubes."

"Did anyone come out?"

She shook her head. "No one. Not a soul."

Ehrich chewed his bottom lip. "Stay here and keep an eye out for any survivors." He had a sinking feeling there would be none.

Dash pulled on Ehrich's sleeve. "What happened?"

"I'm not sure."

"What do we do?"

Ehrich scanned the area. He had no idea what to do or where to go. Mr. Serenity would have been in Purgatory along with the other travellers. The army that would have stood against Ba Tian was either trapped below or worse.

Ehrich had to warn the others. He slipped into an alley away from the bustle of onlookers gawking at the smoke. Dash followed. Ehrich pulled out his communicator and pressed the button. He took a breath, trying to figure out how to break the bad news to Amina and Tesla. Finally, he found the words: "Mr. Tesla. Amina. Do you hear me? I have news."

He waited for a response. Nothing but static. Then Amina's voice came across the receiver. "What is it? We're on the train right now."

"Do you see the smoke from the city?"

Silence.

"Amina?"

"Yes. We do. What's going on? Has the attack begun?"

"No, Amina. Purgatory is burning."

There was no response from the communicator. Ehrich glanced at Dash. He pressed the button again.

"Did you hear me? Purgatory is burning."

Tesla's voice answered. "We heard you, Ehrich. Are you certain?"

"Yes, sir. I'm at one of the entrances. The guard confirmed it. There might have been an explosion below. We don't know for sure, but so far no survivors have come out of this entrance."

"This has to be the work of Ba Tian," Tesla said.

Ehrich pressed the button again. "I don't think so, sir. He didn't seem to know where the refugees were hiding. It might have been an accident."

"Too much of a coincidence. We're going to have to regroup."

Ehrich chewed his bottom lip for a moment. "Sir, we have to warn Edison about the invasion that's coming."

"No one is going to believe us, Ehrich. We're fugitives."

"I think I know someone who can help us."

"Who?"

"Sir, meet us at the nursing home where Charlie is."

"Charlie?"

"Trust me, sir. Go there."

"Very well. We're almost at the station."

—✳WW✳—

Ehrich led Dash through the Bowery streets. Normally, he'd have to be on the lookout for thieves or thugs, but the smoke pouring out of all the portals to Purgatory had captured the attention of the people around him. No one was interested in anything other than the mysterious fire that was burning under their city.

Finally, Ehrich reached his destination. He walked up to the door and glanced around for any hunters. The coast was clear. He knocked three times.

The door opened. Bess was on the other side. She narrowed her eyes but then recognized Ehrich. She peeked into the street then motioned the two boys to enter the house. Charlie sat in a wheelchair in the foyer.

"What are you doing back here?" she demanded.

"We had nowhere else to go."

"What happened to you?"

Ehrich self-consciously touched the wounds Ole Lukoje had inflicted. He recounted the events on Coney Island while Bess rummaged up some clothes that fit the two brothers. Charlie let out a low whistle when Ehrich concluded with the story about the fire.

"I didn't think New York was built on a volcano," Charlie said.

"It's not a volcano. It's actually another city," Dash said before Ehrich could stop him.

"City? What kind of city?" Bess asked.

Ehrich had no choice but to bring his two companions into the fold. He told them everything about the Dimensionals, Ba Tian, and Farrier. They were most interested in the city under New York.

"Purgatory is a place for refugees that have come to this world," Ehrich said. "They aren't welcome up on the surface and they're hiding from a warlord named Ba Tian, who invaded and destroyed their worlds. They've come here for sanctuary and have set up underneath the city to hide from the people of New York and to prepare to fight Ba Tian."

Ehrich then tried his best to answer Charlie and Bess's questions. They had many. "How did they get here?" "What do they want?" "How did they build a city without us knowing it?"

He had answers to some of the questions but not all. "That doesn't matter. What's important is the reason they're here is that Ba Tian attacked and destroyed their worlds. Now he's here to do the same."

"So why hasn't he attacked yet?" Charlie asked.

"I'm not sure. He has Farrier's men, but I think he needs his generals. I think he's going to try to rescue them and I think they're going to try at the execution. We're going to have to warn Thomas Edison."

Charlie nodded. "They'll have to double the shifts on Coney Island. Triple, even."

"If Ba Tian has the exoskeletons, they're going to need an army," Ehrich said. "And with Farrier in the picture, Ba Tian's got one."

Bess interrupted. "Can we negotiate peace with this warlord?"

"I don't think so. I've worked with people who saw what he could do firsthand. I don't think he's the kind who negotiates."

"Then what can we do?" Charlie asked.

"Can you send word to the hunters and let them know something is going to happen at the execution?" Ehrich asked. "Get them to postpone it."

"I don't know if I can. From what I heard, Edison is using this as a major publicity stunt."

Ehrich sighed. "We have to stop Ba Tian."

Bess shook her head. "There are just four of us. What could we possibly do? If this warlord has marshalled forces already, we would need an army."

Dash tugged on Ehrich's jacket. "If we need people to fight, what about the people at the tunnel project?"

"Who?" Charlie asked.

"The travellers who used to work in the tunnels," Dash said. "They seem strong."

Ehrich beamed. "You're right, Dash. They might be the answer. We have to talk to them."

Charlie wheeled himself in front of the pair while Bess crossed her arms. "Hold on there, buddy of mine," said Charlie.

"There is no way you're going into a fight without any backup. Haven't I taught you anything?"

"What are you talking about?"

"I'm coming with you."

Ehrich shook his head. "I'm sorry, Charlie, but I have to move fast."

"You wouldn't believe how fast this thing rolls, and you need someone in case you come across hunters."

Bess nodded. "Charlie can come in handy and I can push him. You'll need us."

"This isn't your fight."

"It is if this warlord means to invade our city," Bess said. "I'm not going to stand by and let that happen."

"What about your other patients?"

"Mrs. Sherman is about to come on shift. Wait until she shows up, then we can go."

Ehrich nodded. "I told Amina and Mr. Tesla to meet us here. We have to wait for them anyway."

"Plus, you look like you need something to eat. Both of you look done in."

Ehrich protested. "I'm fine. We're fine. I'm good. I really think you should stay here, Bess. We can handle it."

She raised herself up. "Ehrich Weisz, I risked my life for you. I let you tie me up and, when I had a chance to turn you over to the authorities, I said nothing. You owe me."

Charlie chuckled. "You got on her bad side. Never get on Bess's bad side. She's right, you know. Without your allies, we're all you have right now, and only a fool would turn down an offer of help."

Ehrich relented. "Okay, okay."

She smiled. "I'll rustle up some grub for you." She headed to the kitchen.

Ehrich walked to the window and stared out, looking for his allies. Instead, he saw the smoke filling the sky. Purgatory, Mr. Serenity, all the travellers were gone.

NEW ALLIES

Stepping off the train, Amina and Tesla stared at the sky that was blackening from the various underground fires around Manhattan. The other passengers jostled them as they made their way down the stairs to the streets below.

"Mr. Serenity was down there," Amina said.

Tesla put his arm around her. "You can't think the worst. We're just seeing smoke right now. We can't be sure of anything that's going on."

"He was all I have left in this world."

"Don't let those thoughts crowd your mind, Amina. We need to keep our focus. Right now, we have to get to Ehrich and Dash. We'll sort out what to do about Purgatory when we find the brothers."

They navigated the streets and headed to the Bowery. They pushed past the throngs of people gathered in the street, staring at the plumes of smoke throughout the city. As Amina made her way past the humans congregating in the street, she could hear the fear and panic overtaking people. Many were talking about the possibility of the demons rioting in New York. Others suggested this might be a prelude to a larger invasion. Some talked about fleeing while a few wanted to marshal forces and fight the demons in the city. The scene was getting ugly and Amina knew this played to Ba Tian's advantage. Without her army, this world would be defenceless against Ba Tian.

She recalled how easy it was for Ba Tian's accomplices to capture them at Coney Island, but then a dreadful thought struck her.

"The ones working with Ba Tian were not crimson soldiers. They were humans."

Mr. Tesla nodded. "Dressed in hunter uniforms. Yes, I had been mulling the same thing since the attack. I didn't recognize any of the hunters, and they seemed older than the usual recruits that Demon Watch uses. We tended to use orphaned teens. They had nothing to lose. These were men and women who seemed to have seen their fair share of battles."

"Who were they?"

"My money is on southerners. The ones who are still bitter over losing the Civil War. Ba Tian had an earlier deal with them. I guess they are sticking to their agreement."

"Then I take that as a good sign."

Tesla cocked his head to one side. "How so?"

"If he's willing to work with humans here, it means he doesn't have his army." She stopped herself when she looked up at the plumes of smoke. Neither did she.

"At this point, Amina, we have to make do with what we have."

"Sir, we have no one now. We're alone against Ba Tian and

whatever forces he has amassed. If he rescues his generals, we are lost."

The lanky man nodded but said nothing.

—••W\/\•—

By the time Amina and Tesla had reached the Bowery, much of New York was in chaos, with volunteer brigades rushing through the streets to fight fires that they could not see. The smoke began to block out the sky. They were close to one of the Purgatory entrances. Smoke billowed out from the cellar door and rose up into the air, choking the firefighters and the curious onlookers.

Amina led Tesla past the crowd and down the alley toward the nursing home where they had tried to trap Kifo. As they drew closer, the door swung open and Ehrich burst outside. He ran to greet the pair.

"I'm so glad to see familiar faces."

"Is Dash all right?" Tesla asked.

"Yes, he's fine. Come in. Come in. We have food."

Tesla straightened up and sniffed the air. "You are a mind reader, Ehrich Weisz. Just what I needed."

"You're always hungry," Amina said.

He ignored her as he entered the house. Ehrich lingered back with her for a moment. "I'm sorry about Mr. Serenity."

She shook her head. "We don't know anything yet. I'm not ready to give up on him."

Ehrich looked down at his feet for a second. "Yes, you're right. He might have survived."

She took his arm. "Is Bess still in the picture?"

He nodded.

"After what we did to her, how can we—"

He cut her off. "She wants to help, Amina. I trust her."

She wanted to say more, but bit her lower lip and followed him into the house.

●─\/\/\─●

Amina picked at what little food was left after Tesla had his fill. He smacked his lips and eyed the cupboards of the kitchen.

Bess laughed. "I'm sorry, Mr. Tesla, but you're going to eat us out of house and home. Mrs. Sherman is going to wonder how a bunch of patients in comas suddenly ate so much."

Tesla rolled his sleeves down and buttoned them. "Ah, yes. I didn't mean to be rude. It's just that you cooked such a delicious repast, I couldn't resist."

Ehrich joked. "You couldn't pass up a half-eaten apple if you found it on the road, sir."

Tesla shot a dirty look at his friend. "I would wash it first." Then he broke into a smile.

Bess ushered the gang out of the kitchen. "Mrs. Sherman is due here soon. You're going to have to clear out before she arrives. I don't want to answer more questions than I have to, and I'm not about to be tied up again."

Ehrich glanced nervously at the others. "Sorry. Again, we're sorry."

She smiled. "And you're going to keep saying that until I believe you."

●─\/\/\─●

The light of day was fading. Gas lighters made their way into the darkened streets to spark up the gas lamps along the Bowery establishments. Ehrich pushed Charlie in the wheelchair. Behind him, Bess, Amina, Dash, and Tesla followed. They had waited until Mrs. Sherman showed up so that the other patients were attended to.

As they went through the streets, the clouds of smoke were lost in the night sky, but Ehrich could smell the acrid stench coming from below. It smelled of burning garbage and sulphur mixed in with a metallic tinge like iron. He shuddered as he continued through the crowds, wondering how many people had died under the city. He shook off the depressing thought and focused on the task at hand. They had to get under the Hudson River tunnel and secure the exoskeletons. Now that they had lost the rebels in Purgatory, the war machines were the only thing that would help them in the battle against Ba Tian.

Ehrich clung to the hope that Ba Tian could only recruit a few humans to his cause and that he couldn't get under the tunnel to retrieve his machines. He convinced himself this was a race to win the war, and this gave his legs the strength to speed along the cobblestone streets of New York until they reached their destination: the Hudson River tunnel project.

He scanned the travellers lingering around fire barrels across the street from the tunnel's perimeter fence. He could sense the tension in the air as the travellers eyed the guards, who seemed to have doubled since Ehrich had last been here.

"There's no way we're going to sneak past those guards," Charlie said.

"Ever the optimist," Bess quipped.

Amina shushed the two. "Quiet. Something doesn't seem right here." She scanned the street for the operatives she had recruited to keep watch. She spotted the meek mouse-faced man who scurried when he walked and twitched his whiskers constantly.

"Elba," she called.

He nearly jumped out of his skin at the sound of his name. He spun around and let out a sharp yip. He relaxed when he saw it was Amina. "You could give a guy some warning before you sneak up on him."

"I'll keep that in mind for next time, Elba. We need to talk. What has been going on here? Where's Renata?"

"Well, it was quiet until the smoke started showing up in the city. We heard rumours it was Purgatory. Renata, her sister is down there. She ran to check. Left me here to keep watch. I'm glad you're here. The humans look tense. I think it's going to get ugly soon."

"Thank you, Elba. You did well."

"Everyone is nervous. More so since the smoke appeared. They fear that the humans are going to turn on us. What do we do? We have nowhere to hide."

"Elba, stay at your post. Watch for anything unusual."

Amina returned to her friends.

"Well?" Ehrich asked.

"Nothing. We might have a chance if we can get into the tunnel now."

Tesla stroked his chin. "It's a risky venture, but what other choice do we have?"

Charlie wheeled forward. "If what I heard from my friends is right, whatever Ba Tian has planned, he's going to do it at the execution."

Amina agreed. "We have to secure the exoskeletons. We still might have a chance."

Ehrich surveyed the guards on the perimeter. "No chance of us storming the place."

Charlie agreed. "They have it locked down tight. I could try to sweet talk them into letting us inspect the place."

Amina grabbed Ehrich. "I can't believe it." Her hands were starting to shake.

"What? What's wrong, Amina?"

She pointed down the street. Ehrich turned and was at a loss for words. Covered in soot and staggering toward them was Mr. Serenity.

DESPERATE TIMES

Amina sprinted toward her mentor with her arms open wide. The weary man could barely lift his head, but he managed to eke out a grim smile when Amina bear-hugged him and lifted him off the ground.

Ehrich and Tesla joined the pair and peppered the man with questions.

"How did you get out, my dear friend?" Tesla asked.

Ehrich cut off the answer. "Were there other survivors?"

"What caused the fire?"

"What happened to everyone else?"

Mr. Serenity waved the pair off and tried to catch his breath. "Give me a moment. Please."

Amina grabbed a wooden crate to use as a chair and helped her friend sit down. Bess wheeled Charlie over with Dash close behind.

"Water. Does anyone have some water?" Amina asked.

Bess rushed off to collect some water from a nearby rain barrel while Amina tended to Mr. Serenity.

"Sir, are you all right?"

He patted her head. "I will be. For now, I require a bit of water and some rest."

"My friend. What happened down there?" Tesla asked.

"To be perfectly honest, I have no idea what happened. I was working on the Infinity Coil in my lab when I heard a series of explosions through the city. The next thing I realized, fires were everywhere. I collected what I could and attempted to go out and help, but the fires were so intense. It was as if the city was melting in front of my eyes. I had no choice. I went back into the building and jumped in the sled.

By the time I got to the surface, I could barely breathe from all the smoke. I sent the sled back, hoping others would follow. I waited, but no one came. I held out hope for as long as I could, but I suspected no one else would be escaping. I thought I'd try to find you at the tunnel project."

"I'm glad you were able to make it out. What do you think caused the explosions?" Tesla asked.

Mr. Serenity scratched his bald head. "It might have been one of the weapons engineers. I know they were testing explosives to use in the war."

"Do you think it was Ba Tian?" Amina asked. "Maybe one of his operatives stole into Purgatory."

"Unlikely, Amina."

Ehrich's eyes narrowed. "Or it could have been Kifo. Maybe he escaped from the Infinity Coil."

Mr. Serenity shook his head. "I doubt it. There's no way the assassin could extricate hims—" A coughing fit interrupted the rest of his thought.

Amina rubbed his back.

Bess returned with water. "Here you go, sir."

Mr. Serenity took the cup from her. "You're too kind. I'm surprised you are here."

"It's a long story, sir," Ehrich said.

"I have all the time in the world now."

Ehrich brought him up to speed about their work on Coney Island, the return of Ba Tian and Farrier, and the recruitment of Charlie and Bess as their allies.

"This is all that is left of our rebel forces," Amina said. "Sir, I fear we have lost the war before we have even gone to battle."

"I'm afraid you might be right. Our army is gone. Perhaps the best thing we can do is flee."

Amina shook her head. "No, I refuse to give up. The only thing we know for sure is that Ba Tian is back in this world. We must secure the exoskeletons under the tunnel."

Mr. Serenity coughed. "You cannot be serious, Amina. Look at us. We're barely enough to take on Ba Tian. Even if we retrieved the exoskeletons, we have no army. You must go."

Dash cleared his throat. "What about my idea? Use the people here." He pointed at the Dimensionals lined up along the buildings outside the project.

Amina chewed her bottom lip. "They're not soldiers. They're civilians."

Dash nodded. "Yes, but they have the numbers we need."

"I'm with Amina," Mr. Serenity said. "They would be lambs to the slaughter."

Tesla crossed his arms. "I'm not so sure, my friend. In desperate times, we must consider all options."

Charlie pointed out. "You can waste your breath arguing or you can ask them. If they turn you down, then you can figure out what to do next. Fretting over what they're going to say isn't going to help any of us."

"Only one way to find out," said Ehrich. Good idea, Dash." He beamed.

Ehrich began to walk toward the Dimensionals. Dash fell in step behind his big brother. They aimed for the purple-skinned woman standing at a barrel fire and holding court over a small group. Ehrich had seen her before and guessed she was the leader.

He extended a hand to her. "Hello. I'm Ehrich Weisz."

She eyed him suspiciously. "What do you want?"

"I've come to you with a chance to make a difference in this world."

"How? Are you going to get me my old job back?"

"Are you the leader of these workers?" Dash asked.

"I'm Hexacate."

"My name is Dash. I'm trying to find my way home and I think you can help."

She smiled. "This is our home now. We must make of it what we will."

"Not for long unless you can help us," Ehrich said.

She raised her hand. Eyes blinked at Ehrich from her fingertips. It reminded him of the boy he had rescued from the general store.

"What do you mean 'not for long'?" Hexacate asked.

"Ba Tian is here." Dash blurted.

"Ba Tian," she spat. "I would love to meet him eye to eye."

"You may have a chance," Ehrich said. "He's preparing to invade this world."

This caught the attention of the people nearby. Some moved closer while others scurried away to pass the word on. Hexacate straightened up to her full height, towering over Ehrich and Dash.

"You've seen him?"

Amina joined the brothers. "Yes, we have. We need an army to fight against him."

She cocked her head. "We're not fighters. We're workers."

Ehrich stepped toward her. "But you also know what Ba Tian can do. This is your chance to stop him and exact your revenge."

"He would decimate us," Hexacate said.

Dash shook his head. "Not if we can even the odds."

A hush fell over the gathering crowd. Hexacate crossed her arms. "What do you have in mind?"

"We can use his machines against him." Dash said.

Hexacate looked from Dash to Ehrich to Amina, confused.

"Tell him, Amina," Dash said.

"Hexacate, what if I told you that below your feet are the very weapons the warlord used to destroy your worlds?" she said. "And all we have to do is get down there and take them."

"I would say that you're mad."

Amina turned to the Amazonian woman. "Is there any chance you will help us?"

Hexacate looked at her workers, now crowding around to hear the conversation. "My first priority is to my people. We can't afford to upset the humans based on what you claim. Prove to us there are weapons below and we might be able to talk, but right now, all we have is your word, and that's not enough."

Amina protested, "We're all in this together. Would you stand idly by while Ba Tian destroys this world?"

"You're the one from Purgatory, aren't you?"

She nodded.

"I thought so. I heard about your paradise under the city where only the chosen are allowed to go. I've seen you come around here. You see how my people have suffered up here. Yet, you never offered us sanctuary in Purgatory. Why not?"

Amina had no answer.

"You don't have to answer. I think we all know why. We weren't worthy of you. Now you need us. You come to us when you have no other options. Do you think that would endear you to us?"

"He will destroy us all," Dash said. "Please. You have to take a stand."

"I've seen what the people in this world are capable of. I suspect Ba Tian has finally met his match. I'm sorry, little boy, but we cannot help you."

Hexacate turned her back. The others grunted approval and walked away.

UNDER THE TUNNEL

A mina paced back and forth in front of the fence. Without the soldiers in Purgatory and with no help from the strikers, her situation seemed hopeless. The guards at the fence weren't about to let them waltz into the Hudson River tunnel project, and time was running out.

Bess was the one who came up with the solution. "Why don't we treat this like the magic act at the Bijou Theatre, Ehrich?"

Charlie wheeled ahead. "Are we going to make the guards disappear?"

She shook her head.

"You want me to perform Metamorphosis?" Ehrich asked.

Mr. Serenity coughed. "We would need the codex and that is down below."

Bess shook her head. "No, I'm talking about what every good illusion needs. Ehrich? You know what I'm talking about, don't you?"

He broke into a smile. "Misdirection."

She snapped her fingers. "Exactly."

Several minutes later, Bess and Dash rolled Charlie's wheelchair along the street toward the gate where the guards were stationed. They began to pick up speed. Bess leaned forward and whispered in Charlie's ear. "You ready?"

"I guess."

They moved faster. He leaned to the right and let his body weight pull the chair to one side. The chair flipped over, sending Charlie to the ground. Bess shrieked as she fell to her knees and tried to pick up Charlie.

Dash waved at the guards to help their fallen friend. "Help, help!"

The guards on the gate turned their attention to the accident and several ran to help right Charlie's chair while Dash ordered them to be careful. The guards along the fence watched the commotion, unaware of Amina, Ehrich, Mr. Serenity, and Tesla slipping toward the fence.

Ehrich pressed his back against the wooden fence and eyed the guards above. The lanterns hanging on poles near the fence cast long shadows and gave Ehrich's team the cover they needed. With Bess and Dash creating a scene and drawing everyone's attention, Ehrich could work quickly and under the cover of night. With a crowbar, he pried a board loose. Amina worked at the other board, opening a wide enough gap for Mr. Serenity and Tesla to crawl through. She held the board open for Ehrich to squeeze through before joining the gang.

On the other side of the fence, the group crept toward the pit. None of the guards noticed as they slipped to the ladders that led down to the tunnels. Bess had done her job and now it was up to Ehrich's team to stop Ba Tian's men from getting the exoskeletons.

Staring down at the flickering torches below, Amina realized just how deep the pit went. She gritted her teeth and slid down the ladder. There was no more time to waste.

They reached the bottom, finally, and grabbed the torches to light up the cavernous pit. Ahead was the entrance into the tunnel proper. About 200 feet in was the airlock used to equalize the pressure of going under the river. The iron door was closed, but there was a crank wheel to open it, just as Ehrich remembered.

They converged on it. Amina spun the wheel around. She pulled hard on the door, sliding it open. A whoosh of air blasted out. It smelled stale, a mixture of deep earth and the ocean. She winced from the smell, but fought it off and peeked inside. The chamber was empty.

Ehrich slid inside and felt along the floor with his foot for the seam that he and Charlie had found when they'd first investigated this place. He moved methodically across the floor in front of the opening, moving to one wall and then the next, until finally he felt his toe catch on a notch in the floor. The others entered the chamber behind him as he lifted the trap door that led into the sub-tunnel. Ehrich stuck his torch into the opening and waited for his eyes to adjust. The heat from the flames warmed his face and illuminated the narrow and rough tunnel.

"This is supposed to take us to the cavern with the exoskeletons," he said. Ehrich motioned the others to follow. "It's this way. Come on."

Mr. Serenity coughed. "We have to extinguish the torches or else they will see us coming."

"How will you be able to see?" Tesla asked.

"It's a straight line to the other side," Ehrich said. We just have to keep our hands on the wall."

They doused the torches, plunging the team into darkness. Ehrich led the way, feeling his way along the rough rock. He seemed to be inching forward for what felt like an eternity as his eyes adjusted to the dark. A dim light shone from the end of the tunnel.

He began to quicken the pace as the light grew closer. He stopped at the mouth of the tunnel. The source of the light was coming from below. He waited until the others caught up before he cautiously leaned out of the tunnel to peer below.

Arrayed in rows and columns were Ba Tian's exoskeleton machines. Artificial light from rocks around the perimeter provided enough illumination for Ehrich to see the weaponry that the warlord had used to destroy worlds. Amina joined him and gasped, covering her mouth.

Something, however, didn't look right. The arrangement of the exoskeletons was perfect, but a section of the cavern had a large number of exoskeletons missing. Everything else was so uniform, it struck her as odd that the one section would be bare. The slow realization dawned on her. Many of the machines had already been taken out of the tunnel.

BETRAYAL

A mina led the group down into the cavern to the exoskeletons. She wrestled with the notion that Ba Tian would side with the humans in this dimension, which gave her hope that he had not amassed his soldiers in this world yet. She fretted, however, that even a handful of soldiers equipped with the exoskeletons could lay waste to New York. She had to find a way to even the odds, and the remaining machines were her only option.

Behind her, Tesla marvelled at the rows and rows of iron behemoths. The exoskeletons towered over him, standing at least twice as high as the lanky scientist. A clear bubble cockpit sat in the chest of the human-shaped machine. Its arms were loaded with weapons to fire razor-sharp discs. Its metal legs powered the heavy machine forward and backward. The back of the machine was loaded with gears and rods that seemed to link to the exoskeleton's extremities.

Tesla chirped, "Imagine the technology that went into constructing such devices. The precision that was required. What powers these, Mr. Serenity?"

At the rear of the group, the rotund man answered, "I think they are powered by servos in the back of the unit. I can't be sure, but I think they are powered by some kind of mechanical engine. Perhaps steam powered. I'd have to take a closer look to be sure."

"Imagine if I could convert these to my Tesla generators. They would be unstoppable."

"Would you have time to do this, Mr. Tesla?" Amina asked.

"If I had a month, perhaps, but we're dealing with days and hours. I suspect we'll need all the time we have to learn how to operate the equipment."

She nodded then headed to the nearest exoskeleton machine and popped open the hatch on the underside of the bubble cockpit. She climbed up and surveyed the series of pedals and levers within the cockpit right across from the harness seat at the back of the cockpit. She took note of the controls, assessing how hard it would be to operate the exoskeleton. She didn't have time to figure out the nuances. She just needed to know how to make it walk and shoot.

Tesla strolled toward the open area where several workstations with various pieces of equipment were set up. He moved close enough to one table to take note of the weaponry. He picked up a razor-sharp tael, a flat round disk that could fit into the palm of his hand. The disk had a square hole in the centre, which Tesla guessed was for mounting in the weapon. He flicked the disk at the wooden table and it imbedded itself in the heavy wood with ease.

Marty Chan

Amina climbed down and gathered the others around her. Tesla sized up the machine next to him and spoke first. "How will we move these out of the tunnel?"

"I'm sure there has to be some way to the river," Amina said. "These units must be amphibious."

Ehrich nodded. "I'll search the cavern for the entrance to the river. Might be easier to get people down here to drive these things out."

"We have to convince them to come down here first," Amina said.

"I'm sure Charlie will be able to convince them. He's got a way with people."

"I hope you're right. With just the four of us, that's not enough to face off against Ba Tian and his men."

Mr. Serenity climbed into the cockpit of a nearby machine.

"Oh, good," Amina said. "It looks like Mr. Serenity is going to show us how to work these things."

The hatch clanged shut and the machine whirred to life, spinning its torso around to face the group. Amina was impressed that her mentor was able to take control so quickly. Maybe it wasn't going to take that long to figure out how to operate these things. She gave her mentor a thumbs-up. "How did you figure it out so quickly?" she asked.

Mr. Serenity didn't answer. Instead, he cracked a grin as the exoskeleton arm lowered and the turret whirred to life. Amina tried to make sense of what he was doing, aiming a live weapon right at her group.

Suddenly, the weapon burst into fire. Disks erupted from the gun on the machine's metal arm. Ehrich dove out of the way, sliding behind one of the exoskeletons. Amina reacted a fraction too slowly and felt sharp searing pain across her shoulder as one of the disks slashed her. She pushed Tesla to the ground and ran for cover behind one of the other exoskeletons.

Mr. Serenity's machine stumbled forward like a dinosaur in search of its prey. More disks flew, clanking off the armour of the parked exoskeletons.

Amina screamed, "Stop it! What are you doing?"

Behind the cockpit glass, Mr. Serenity howled with laughter as he pulled the levers to and fro and unleashed another volley at Amina and Tesla. They were safe behind one of the iron giants, but Mr. Serenity wasn't finished yet. His machine lumbered toward them and knocked the exoskeletons over. They crashed into each other and tumbled down like dominoes. Amina and Tesla scrambled from their positions of safety to keep from being crushed. Another volley of disks screamed through the air.

Then Mr. Serenity's machine spun around and took aim at the tunnel entrance. A volley of disks was launched at the rock overhead, followed by a *whomp* as a projectile fired from the back of the unit. An explosion rocked the cavern as loose debris showered the area. Rocks were tumbling down and blocking off the tunnel entrance. Amina screamed at Tesla to climb into an exoskeleton. She hauled herself into the cockpit of a nearby unit with Tesla's help then reached down and pulled the lanky man up.

Both squeezed inside the cockpit. They tried to manipulate the controls to make the thing stand up, but nothing worked. Amina glared out the cockpit at Mr. Serenity's machine. It lumbered toward Ehrich's position. She frantically pushed and pulled the levers until her exoskeleton lurched forward. Tesla found the controls for the gun turret and raised the exoskeleton's arm. Disks shot out of the gun and pinged harmlessly off the back of Mr. Serenity's machine.

The iron behemoth swivelled around and returned fire. None of the disks penetrated the bubble. She grinned at Tesla, who pointed through the glass.

"Ehrich's getting into one of the exoskeletons. We have to keep Mr. Serenity distracted."

She nodded. She pressed the pedals and the unit lumbered toward Mr. Serenity's exoskeleton. The two iron giants exchanged fire, but neither scored any hits. Meanwhile, Ehrich climbed safely into his cockpit and fumbled with the controls.

Mr. Serenity grinned at Amina and Tesla from inside his cockpit as he unleashed another volley at them. Cracks in the glass began to fracture. A few more hits and they'd be sliced up. She returned fire.

More cracks on the bubble glass appeared as the rocks from above rained down on them. Tesla gripped her arm, pulling her down as the first disk penetrated the cockpit and struck the seat just over her head. They were exposed now. Amina turned the machine to the side, letting the iron hull take the brunt of the next volley. She peered out the side.

Ehrich's unit joined the battle. He had figured out the controls. The two iron exoskeletons clashed. One brought down an arm on top of the other, pounding it several times. That one then fired disks into the cockpit of the other. Ehrich's machine teetered for a moment. Mr. Serenity's exoskeleton shoved it hard and knocked it to the ground.

Amina cranked her unit around and fired at Mr. Serenity's exoskeleton. The disks pinged off, but it was enough to drive the exoskeleton away from Ehrich's prone unit.

Mr. Serenity's machine lumbered toward the far end of the tunnel as rocks continued to rain down around them. The exoskeleton lowered itself into the water until it was completely submerged. He had found a way out of the tunnel. Amina realized the only way that Mr. Serenity could do all of this was if he wasn't really her mentor. The slow realization of the truth settled upon her. Her friend had been possessed. He was now Kifo.

She gripped the controls, unsure of what to do. A few feet away, Ehrich's unit rose to its feet. Rocks rained down on both exoskeletons. Inside the cockpit, Amina felt the reverberations.

Tesla shouted, "Follow him! Into the river. It's our only escape!"

His voice shook her out of her daze and she applied pressure to the pedals, moving the machine ahead. She glanced to the side and spotted Ehrich in his cockpit, fumbling with the controls. She waved at him to follow. He nodded. Another rock smacked into the cockpit and the hole that the disk had made grew larger.

"We're going to take in water," she yelled.

Tesla shimmied out of his jacket and bundled it up. He pressed it against the hole in the glass as the unit entered the water. Amina took one last look back as the cavern collapsed on top of the remaining exoskeletons. Their only hope of defeating Ba Tian was gone.

A NEW ARMY

Charlie, Bess, and Dash kept watch over the Hudson River tunnel. The travellers were tense, watching the fence and the bustle of activity among the guards. A few moments earlier, the earth had shaken and a loud rumble had filled the night air. Now, dust rose up from the work site, choking out many of the guards and a few of the travellers. Something had happened in the tunnel.

Charlie wheeled his chair forward. "We have to get closer to the site. See what's what."

Bess pulled him back. "They're not going to let us in, Charlie."

Dash shook his head. "We can't leave Ehrich down there. We have to help."

"The kid's right, Bess. We might be the only ones who can save them."

She steeled herself, stepping in front of the two of them and holding her ground. As much as she wanted to run to the work site and help Ehrich and the others, she also had to be the reasonable one. Any attempt to storm the gate would trigger a skirmish that would most likely end poorly.

"We can't do nothing, Bess," Charlie said.

She put her hands on her hips. "We're not going to be any help to them if we get ourselves tossed in jail. Right now, all we can do is keep watch."

Dash argued, "Keep watch on what? It's pretty clear that something has gone wrong in the tunnel. Ehrich and the others might be under attack. We have to save them."

"With what, Dash? We don't have any weapons and we have no army, and we don't know for sure what's really going on at the work site."

Suddenly, shouts from the guards caught everyone's attention. Shots fired in the night. Now Bess was the one to run to the fence. Dash pushed Charlie after her. The noise also attracted the travellers, who surged forward as curious onlookers to the chaos unfolding on the other side of the fence.

When Bess arrived at the fence, she craned her neck to peer over the guards clustered on the other side of the gate. They were all pointing at two exoskeletons rising from the water and shambling onto the shore. The guards took aim at the hulking machines stomping toward them and fired their Teslatron rifles. The exoskeletons continued to advance.

Some of the travellers screamed in recognition. "Ba Tian's army. They are launching an attack. Run!"

Bess glanced around her as chaos erupted. The panicked travellers at the fence now tried to push their way through the crowd and run away. The ones further back were still surging forward to get a better look at the commotion. The guards continued to fire on the machines with no effect.

Charlie took charge. He wheeled himself around to face the travellers. "Listen up! All of you! These guards are our only line of defense. We need to be ready if they fail. Arm yourselves with whatever you can find. So far, there are only two exoskeletons. We can flank them and take them down, but only if you calm down."

His voice carried over the crowd and a hush fell over everyone. Hexacate strode forward and motioned everyone to back away. "The boy is right. We must defend ourselves against these attackers. Those of you in the rear, find weapons."

The travellers furthest away from the fence peeled away and scoured the streets for weapons.

"We're going to get cut down if we all stand here by the fence," Charlie said. "We have to clear the way. We need to sneak behind them. Far ends of the fences. Either end. First to slip through takes on the machines. Make sense?"

Hexacate nodded. "If you're not a fighter, back away from the fence. Find shelter. The rest of you, split off left and right. Take either side of the fence. Be ready to rush ahead."

The guards took aim at the oncoming machines. The energy bolts sizzled against the iron hulls. The exoskeletons drew even closer. Behind Charlie, the travellers organized, clearing a path as they moved to the left and right. Charlie gripped the wheels of his chair, bracing for what was to come.

The guards fired another volley of energy bolts. No effect on the iron giants, but a huge impact on the nerve of the guards. They broke ranks, dropped their weapons, and scattered. They pushed each other out of the way as they fled through the gate, running past Charlie, Bess, and Dash.

Not a soul remained within the confines of the fenced-off

property. The exoskeletons advanced closer to Charlie and his friends. Then they came to a dead stop. Silence filled the air. Charlie tensed, ready for a fight.

The lead unit lowered its metal arms. Inside the cockpit sat Amina and Tesla. The other one came around to reveal that the pilot within was Ehrich.

Charlie raised his hand to the others. "Hold your fire! They're friends!"

Hexacate motioned her travellers to stand down as she made her way to the gate. She shook her head as Ehrich, Amina, and Tesla climbed out of the cockpits.

"They certainly know how to make an entrance," she grumbled.

Charlie beamed. "That they do. That they do."

Bess rushed to Ehrich and wrapped her arms around him. Dash followed suit. The travellers gathered around the gate, craning their necks for a better view.

"What happened down there?" Bess asked. "What was that ruckus?"

Ehrich explained, "We tried to get the exoskeletons, but Ba Tian's men beat us to it. They have a good number of them. The rest are buried under the tunnel."

"What? How?"

"Hey. Where's Mr. Serenity?" Dash asked.

Ehrich fell silent and cast a glance at Amina. She took a breath before answering. "I'm afraid that we have lost Mr. Serenity."

"How?" Dash asked.

She lowered her voice. "Kifo."

"He's back?"

She nodded but could not find the words. Tesla put his arm around her.

Ehrich explained, "We think Kifo possessed Mr. Serenity. He turned on us in the tunnel and brought the rocks down. He climbed into one of the exoskeletons and slipped away into the river. He's probably going to rendezvous with Ba Tian and the rest of the forces."

"We're going to have to stop them," Tesla said.

"But we don't have the time to dig any exoskeletons out," Ehrich said. "We can't face off against Ba Tian with two of these. We need an army."

Hexacate strode forward. "I never would have believed it if I hadn't seen it with my own eyes. You have his weapons."

"Yes, but the rest are buried under the tunnel. There is no way we can recover them."

"That is unfortunate."

"You see that Ba Tian is here now, don't you?"

She nodded. "But that is not our problem."

"Yes, but when the fight comes to your doorstep, it will be," Ehrich pointed out. He began to walk away.

As he did, a young boy rushed to Hexacate and wrapped his arms around her leg. "Momma. Are we going to have to run again?"

"Gur-Rahim, I will not let anything happen to you."

Ehrich took a second look at the boy. Something about him seemed familiar. He couldn't place the kid, but he knew he had seen him before. It was only when the boy lifted his hands to reveal the two eyes on his fingertips that Ehrich remembered. He was the boy he had rescued from the general store.

"Gur-Rahim," Ehrich said. "I thought it was you."

The boy turned to Ehrich and cocked his head to the side. "Do I know you?"

Ehrich realized he had been in disguise earlier. There would be no way the boy could recognize him unless ... Ehrich reached behind the boy's ear and pulled out a coin. The boy's eyes widened with wonder.

"It's not the candy I gave you in the store, but maybe you'll be able to buy what you want."

The boy squinted at Ehrich's face, piecing together his memory. "It's you. You look different."

"I was in disguise earlier."

"How do you know this man, Gur-Rahim?"

"Momma, you remember what I told you about the attack in the store. This is the one who rescued me."

Hexacate straightened up. "Are you certain, my son?"

He nodded. "First, he made candy appear magically. Then when the people turned on me, he pulled me out of the store."

"Why would you do that?" Hexacate stared at Ehrich. "You didn't even know him."

Ehrich shrugged. "When I see someone in need of help, I don't decide based on who they are or how I know them. I just help."

Gur-Rahim tossed the coin up. "If it wasn't for him, I don't know what those people would have done to me."

Hexacate took a long look at her son, then tousled his hair. "Go on and play. I have to talk to our friend here."

The young boy smiled at Dash. "You want to see my collection of rocks?"

Dash glanced at Ehrich, who nodded. "Sure. I'd love to."

Hexacate watched the two boys go. "That boy is the only family I have left in this or any world. He means everything to me."

"He was just in the wrong place at the wrong time."

"It was a good thing you were there to save him."

"I'm not talking about the store. I'm talking about this world, Hexacate. He's here and he's going to witness the death of another world. Or worse, he's going to be part of the destruction. Unless you and your people are willing to lift a hand to help."

"We have no means to fight the exoskeletons."

"We have two of them. It's a start."

"It's not our battle," she said.

"And it's not his, either, but he's a part of it whether you want him to be or not."

"I owe nothing to these people," she said, pursing her lips.

"I know that, but you owe your son a better life than one where you flee from one ravaged world to the next, don't you think?"

In the distance, Gur-Rahim picked up rocks and handed them to Dash. A knot of guilt tightened in Ehrich's stomach. He tried to ignore it as he watched his brother playing with the boy as if they were back in their home world and none of this had ever happened.

Amina regained her composure and pulled away from Tesla. "Hexacate, you do nothing and we are ruined. It's time to act. You can't stand on the sidelines anymore. You have to fight. You don't and we're all dead. All of us—"

Tesla put his arm around her again and pulled her away.

Ehrich straightened up, standing as tall as he could to meet Hexacate's eyes. "What's your decision?"

She looked from him to her son with Dash. Then she fixed her gaze back on Ehrich. "What do you want us to do?"

"Thank you," Ehrich said. "We have to go to Coney Island first. If Ba Tian succeeds in getting the generals, he'll be able to launch a full-scale assault on this city."

Charlie piped up. "No. We have to go to Devil's Island and warn them. We need more bodies to fight."

"There's no way they're going to listen to us, Charlie," Ehrich said. "We're still on their wanted list."

"They might listen to me. I could warn the hunters if someone gets me to the island."

"Are you sure they'll listen to you?" Ehrich asked. "It's been a while since you were on the force."

"I'm pretty sure there will be a few veterans who remember me. At least they'll be willing to give me the time of day."

"We can't send him alone," Bess said.

"We can't send any of the travellers, and Amina and I need to lead the forces against Coney Island. That only leaves you, Bess," Ehrich said.

The slim girl scowled. "You think you're taking me out of harm's way. Think again."

He shook his head. "We need the hunters on our side. It's the only thing that will keep Ba Tian from getting everything he needs."

Charlie pointed out, "If I could travel on my own power, I'd go on my own, but it would be nice to have a friendly face with me in case things go south."

Bess stamped her foot down on the pavement. "There is no way you're taking me out of this fight. I'm going with you to Coney Island to face off against this warlord. If he's coming to destroy my city, I want to be able to stand up to him."

"We need the firepower of the hunters," Charlie said.

"No. Most of them will be guarding the execution site. With the sabotage Ehrich told me about, I'm pretty sure Thomas Edison isn't going to leave anything to chance. It's most likely that Devil's

Island will have a few hunters while the rest will be guarding the prisoners. That's where Ba Tian is going to attack and there's where we will have the best chance of ending this invasion."

Ehrich began to argue, but Charlie cut him off. "You know this firebrand might just have a point. If I were in charge of Demon Watch, I would make damn sure that we had enough bodies to watch the generals. Ain't no reason to launch an attack on Devil's Island if all the generals are in the city."

"Charlie agrees with me. We have to stay together if we want any chance of beating Ba Tian."

Ehrich sighed. "Okay, okay. You win, Bess. We'll go together."

Dash and Gur-Rahim returned. Amina and Tesla joined them. She nodded at Ehrich. "Sorry, my anger spilled over."

"Water under the bridge," he said. "We have to focus on Coney Island."

"What are we going to do, Ehrich?" Dash asked.

Ehrich placed a hand on his shoulder and said, "We're going to fight."

"If we leave a small force here with the two exoskeletons, they might be able to clear away the rubble in the tunnel and get the other machines," Hexacate said. "That might give us an edge against the forces."

Charlie nodded. "There's no way we can take the units with us to Coney Island without creating a ruckus. We'd spend more time trying to fight off New Yorkers to get to the train. We're better off going with what we have."

Amina shook her head. "Those exoskeletons are devastating. We're going to have to be strategic about this. I'd be more comfortable if we could bring at least one of the units with us. That could buy us some time and cover against the army."

"Then let's make it our priority to secure one of their units when we reach the island," Bess suggested.

"Are you sure we can't take the units with us?" Hexacate asked.

"They won't fit on the train," Tesla pointed out.

"How do you think Ba Tian is moving them?" Dash asked.

"Most likely the same way we escaped from the tunnel. He's probably piloting them underwater."

"Then let's do the same. Maybe we can catch up to Kifo. How fast do they move, Mr. Tesla?"

"I don't know the top speed, but they are swift."

"We'll be able to launch a secondary assault from the beach," Hexacate said. "And right now, we need all the help we can get."

The others agreed. Hexacate ordered two of her people to climb into the exoskeletons. Once they were familiar with the controls, they piloted the units into the river while the rest of the crew marched to the nearest train station. Dawn was starting to break as they reached the platform with the contingent of Dimensionals. Only vendors and deliverymen were awake at this hour, giving the troop the freedom to climb onto the platform without any notice. They headed up to the platform to await the arrival of the train. If other New Yorkers arrived, they'd have to stand in line at the bottom of the stairs. Hexacate's people had filled the stairwell body to body. With the weapons they took from the Hudson River guards, they were a force to be reckoned with. Ehrich only hoped that these fighters would be enough.

They boarded the train, filling every seat and every car. The train wheeled slowly ahead and picked up steam, taking them to their ultimate destination: Coney Island.

THE INVASION BEGINS

The scene at Coney Island was not what Ehrich had expected. As the train pulled into the station, the sun was rising and the rays of light reflected off two exoskeletons stationed at the bottom of the platform. Ehrich scanned the cockpits for Kifo, but he was not there. The machines swivelled toward the train and raised their gun turrets.

Ehrich bolted up and shouted, "We have to get off the train now!"

The other passengers screamed as they saw what he had seen, and a stampede of travellers rushed for the exit. Suddenly, a volley of disks strafed the car. Glass shattered. A few of Hexacate's travellers fell to their knees, clutching bleeding wounds. They were under attack! Ehrich pushed the people out the other side of the train, which was still rolling to the station. The fall to the ground below would hurt but they would live. The steady rat-a-tat of the disks piercing the train cars filled the air, punctuated with the screams of the injured. Ehrich grabbed Dash and together they jumped off.

Only two exoskeletons were wreaking havoc on the train. Ehrich dreaded what would happen when they faced an entire troop of these devastating machines.

Amina joined him on the ground under the elevated rails, bringing with her some of the survivors. Tesla was further down the tracks with Hexacate and another pack of travellers. Ehrich signalled the other group to stay low. Above, more Dimensionals were leaping out of the train, which was now screeching to a halt. Sparks flew from the steel wheels grating on the tracks.

Some of the people who had fallen to the ground were not getting back up. Their bodies were lacerated with disks. The exoskeletons had done their job.

Amina gritted her teeth. "They're cutting off Coney Island from anyone who might be able to help. That must mean the generals are already here for the execution."

Ehrich agreed. "We have to move now. Maybe we can skirt around these guards and rush to the site."

"I want to come with you," Dash said.

"No. It's too dangerous."

Dash insisted. "No more dangerous than sitting out in the open here. I can help."

"No, you'd just get in the way."

"I can operate the exoskeletons," Dash said.

Amina shook her head. "The boardwalk offers no cover. We could use those two exoskeletons. If we can distract the pilots, maybe a small group can take over the units."

Ehrich nodded. He raised a hand to signal Hexacate. He

pointed at the exoskeletons stationed at the bottom of the train platform and used his fingers to signal her group to fire upon the machines. She nodded and began ordering her people to take up positions under the tracks.

Amina instructed the travellers. "Focus your fire on the exoskeletons. Buy us enough time to get behind them. Then hold your fire if you see us making our way to the units. Understood?"

The Dimensionals nodded. Amina and Ehrich edged away from the group and moved under the tracks as the air began to sizzle with the energy bursts from the Teslatron rifles. The battle had begun. Disks screamed through the air and clanked off the pillars of the overhead rail lines. Above, the survivors of the initial attack had fired down on the units as well. Ehrich smiled grimly, glad that some of the people on the train were still around. He checked back for Dash, Charlie, and Bess. They had found safe positions.

Amina led the way to the exoskeleton on the left, leaving the one closer to the train to engage Hexacate's travellers. Her group closed the distance, but the machine began to swivel toward them. Amina and her allies were caught out in the open. She sprinted to close the distance, but the pilot spotted her and took aim with the gun turret.

Ehrich tried to pull her away but he, too, was caught in the crosshairs. Suddenly, an energy bolt struck the unit on the side. Ehrich turned to see the source. Bess and Dash were shoving Charlie's wheelchair ahead at full speed while the pale young man fired shot after shot from his Teslatron. The energy bolts lit up the shield of the cockpit. The pilot frantically pulled and pushed at the controls to spin the turret around to meet the new enemy.

Ehrich and Amina sprinted under the exoskeleton. Ehrich reached up and spun the wheel of the hatch and yanked it open. Amina aimed her pistol at the pilot and fired two darts. One pinged off the seat while the other struck the pilot's leg. He seized up in his seat and the exoskeleton's arms dropped to its sides. He convulsed in the harness until he passed out.

Ehrich launched Amina up into the cockpit and she pushed the wounded pilot out. He slammed the hatch shut as the unit lumbered toward the other exoskeleton. Ehrich used Amina's unit as cover as it marched closer and closer to its companion. When it was a few feet away, Amina launched a volley of shots into the back of the iron behemoth. Ehrich sprinted toward the underbelly of the second exoskeleton as it was swivelling around to face off against Amina's unit.

The two iron giants grappled each other's arms and pushed each other back. The Dimensionals charged from their positions to assault the unit. Ehrich reached the hatch and spun it open. Inside, the pilot was too busy concentrating on Amina's unit to notice him until it was too late. Ehrich fired his dynatron pistol once and struck the pilot in the calf. The erupting electricity stunned the pilot and the machine went inert.

The travellers cheered as they charged ahead. Charlie, Bess, and Dash rushed to Ehrich and helped him pull the pilot out of the cockpit. They stripped the man of his weapons and trussed him up alongside the one Amina had kicked out of her cockpit.

Hexacate took stock of her people. They had already lost a third of their numbers from the train attack. The engine was dead and the train blocked the tracks. There would be no one else coming into Coney Island. They were on their own against the warlord's forces.

"We need to march on the demonstration site and see if we can stop Ba Tian," Ehrich told the others. "Now that you've seen how we got in the machines, that's what you have to do."

"Who is going to operate the units?" Tesla asked.

"I will do it," Hexacate said. "What do I need to know?"

Her son rushed up beside her. "I will help you, Mamma."

She beamed and hoisted him up into her arms. "You? What do you think you can do, little one?"

"I can help," he said.

Ehrich smiled. "And the cockpit is probably the safest place for him."

"All right. Let's get inside, then."

"What about me?" Charlie asked. "I don't want to slow you guys down."

"It would be a tight squeeze," she said. "But you should fit in one of these things."

He pulled out the communication device. "I have a better idea. I can find high ground and relay troop positions to you, Ehrich. What do you say?"

"Great idea!" He flashed a quick glance at Dash.

Charlie picked up on the hint. "But I'm going to need a second pair of eyes and someone to push me. Dash, you think you could help?"

Dash's face lit up. "You bet."

Bess shook her head. "They'll need someone to cover them. Hand me a pistol."

Ehrich smiled admiringly at her before handing over a pistol. "You know how to shoot one of these things?"

She tapped the barrel. "This is the deadly end. Point and pull the trigger. That about cover it?"

"Well, you have to hit the target."

She smiled. "My dad taught me how to hunt when I was eight. I won't miss. I won't let anything happen to Charlie or Dash."

"I wouldn't stand in her way, Ehrich. The Dimensionals should run from her if she gets her temper up."

She laughed and pushed Charlie away with Dash scouting ahead. Ehrich watched them go, hoping they would be safe. Behind him, Amina and Hexacate climbed into their cockpits and fired up their iron machines.

—◦◦◦◦◦—

Once they were ready, they marched on the execution site. Amina and Hexacate led their group to the back side of the execution stage while Ehrich led his forces toward the front of it.

As his troop drew near, Ehrich saw that they were already too late. Two horse-drawn paddy wagons were parked beside the stage. Ehrich glimpsed crimson hands clutching the bars of the wagon windows and guessed the occupants were Ba Tian's generals awaiting their fate. Edison's hunters took cover on the other side of the stage, right next to the generators. The hunters fired at a couple of dozen exoskeletons marching toward the stage. Ehrich scanned the cockpits for any sign of Kifo, now in Mr. Serenity's body, believing he would be leading the charge. He couldn't see the assassin.

Another dozen exoskeletons were lumbering to the right of the stage to flank the hunters. By a rough count, Ehrich estimated that maybe three dozen exoskeletons were about to attack. He scanned the shore, half-expecting to see more machines waiting to charge in and finish off the dwindling defenses that Edison had set up around the demonstration site. Where were the others? He scanned the empty beach for Kifo and other soldiers.

Nothing but ocean. He had hoped the two travellers who piloted the exoskeletons from the Hudson River would have arrived, but he saw no sign of them.

He pulled out the communication device. "Charlie, are you guys in position?"

"Almost. Wheels are stuck. Dash and Bess are pushing but it's slow going."

"The main force seems to be in front of the stage with another dozen working their way behind. They're concentrating their fire on the guards around the two paddy wagons. Do you see any more of Ba Tian's forces?"

"Hold on. Dash is going to get a better view."

He waited for several seconds for Charlie to reply. Time inched by as the sound of energy bolts and the scream of razor-sharp disks erupted in the morning air. The hunters were clearly losing the battle, being outgunned by the massive machines. It wouldn't take long for Ba Tian to overcome the forces and take back the generals.

Finally, Charlie responded. "No sign of any other enemy forces. The best attack is on the dozen exoskeletons moving behind the stage."

"Thanks, Charlie. Wait until my forces are in position, then tell Amina to launch an offensive on the smaller group. I'll engage the main forces and keep them occupied. Let me know if anyone comes up behind us."

"Understood, Ehrich."

"Stay safe," Bess said.

Ehrich pocketed the device and rallied the forces to charge

at the main force of exoskeletons. He concentrated the group's fire power on the exoskeletons lumbering toward the generators. The hunters were falling back and losing many of their numbers to the flying disks.

He moved in with the travellers to a position behind the machines. He then pressed his communicator.

"Charlie. We're ready. Tell Amina."

"I read you, Ehrich."

—∿∿—

A few moments later, a fresh assault began on the exoskeletons trying to flank the hunters. Amina in her unit and Hexacate in hers led the charge toward the back end of the execution stage.

Ba Tian's exoskeletons swivelled to confront the new enemy. This was the distraction Ehrich had hoped for. He led the charge to the underbelly of the machines in front of the stage. He waited until everyone had found a position at the hatch, then he gave the signal. One person opened the hatch while the other fired into the cockpit and took out the pilots. Ehrich climbed into a unit and waved for the others to do the same. Inside the cockpits, travellers desperately tried to figure out the controls. Some were more successful than others, but taking out a chunk of the iron troops gave the hunters a fighting chance.

Ehrich directed his gun turret at the rest of the units in front of the stage. Volley after volley strafed the exoskeletons. His troops had figured out how to fire upon the enemy and they joined the firefight from their standing positions. The rest of the Dimensionals rushed to get under some of the machines near the generators. They had lost the element of surprise, but they

Marty Chan

still tried to get under the iron giants. Many fell under the volley of disks. Ehrich directed his turret at the units and provided some cover fire. Two travellers made it to the underbelly of one of the exoskeletons and hauled the pilot out. It was a small victory, but at least they were making progress.

The other travellers spread out and tried to hijack more of the exoskeletons, but they couldn't close the distance. Instead, they nestled into positions and fired on the enemies. The hunters were confused, unsure of who to shoot at. When they saw two of the travellers sneak under a machine and crack the hatch open, they took action. While the exoskeletons were turning to fire upon the travellers, some of the hunters moved into position under the units and pulled open the hatches. The exoskeleton pilots were being attacked from front and back. It wouldn't take much longer for the iron troops to fall.

Ehrich's moment of victory was cut short when the communicator squawked at him. "They're moving on you!"

He faced three exoskeletons charging on his position.

His communicator squawked again. Charlie's voice shouted, "On your right. Turn. Turn."

Ehrich spun the controls to confront a charging exoskeleton. In the cockpit of the approaching machine sat his former commander, George Farrier.

CAPTURED

Ehrich steeled himself and prepared for battle against overwhelming odds. He took aim at the cockpit of Farrier's unit and unleashed a volley, then he pedalled his machine into action and ran to meet the oncoming assault. The ping of metal disks bouncing off his armour was deafening, but he narrowed his gaze and pushed ahead to take on the commander's exoskeleton.

They clashed in the middle of the battle. The giant machine arms grappled one another as they tried to get leverage on their opponent. Farrier had more experience at the controls and was overpowering Ehrich's unit, but Ehrich wasn't going to go down easily. He snaked his unit's iron arm out and fired a round of disks into his opponent's arm. The sharp disks cut into the servos of the iron arm and rendered it useless. It now dangled from the exoskeleton body.

Farrier's unit pummelled the cockpit glass of Ehrich's machine until cracks appeared. It wouldn't be long before the glass would break and Ehrich would be defenseless. He blocked the next blow with both the exoskeleton hands and tried to pedal forward to drive Farrier's unit into the ground. Out of the corner of his eye, he could see Farrier's other units rush past him and engage his comrades. They were not prepared for this kind of pitched battle and he knew that the odds were against them.

He saw hope, however, when two stray exoskeletons lumbered up from the beach, dripping wet as if they had emerged from the ocean. The travellers from the tunnel project had arrived in the nick of time. They blasted their rounds at the enemy and brought down two machines.

One of the exoskeletons raised a turret at Farrier's unit. Farrier howled in the cockpit as he tried to pull the controls and confront the new enemy.

Ehrich slipped out of his harness and opened the hatch, dropping to the ground. The distraction was all he needed to slip under Farrier's unit and pull open his hatch. Ehrich drew his pistol and fired a dart into the man's chest. Farrier was stunned and his unit went limp.

Ehrich waved at the other unit to engage the enemy. The behemoth turned toward the main forces and lumbered off while Ehrich hauled the one-legged man out of the cockpit. A few feet away, Tesla directed two travellers to join him in helping Ehrich.

Tesla rushed to his friend's side. "Are you injured?"

"No, sir. I'm fine. A lot better than Farrier, anyway."

Tesla smiled. "A good catch."

Ehrich slapped the unconscious man's face several times. "Wake up! Up!"

Groggy, the southerner barely mumbled an answer. "What? What?"

"We know you're working with Ba Tian. Where is Kifo? Where are the rest of the exoskeleton forces? Tell me!"

Farrier began to regain some of his self-control. "I don't know what you're talking about."

"You see those hunters over there? I throw you to them and you'll be joining the generals on the execution line."

"That doesn't matter anymore."

"Why not?" Tesla asked.

Farrier chuckled. "Because it's over for you and your forces."

"We're already getting the upper hand on your units, Farrier," Ehrich said. "Take a look around. You'll see that your machines are starting to lose the war. Between our people and the hunters, it's only going be a matter of time before we rout your men."

"You're too late, kid. Far too late."

Ehrich ordered the travellers, "Pick him up. Follow me."

"What are you doing?" Farrier asked.

Ehrich motioned the travellers to push the man forward, half-carrying him toward the hunters who had their rifles trained on the group.

"Take a good look at who we pulled out of the units attacking you. Recognize him?!"

The hunters looked at each other, puzzled. Then they peered at the struggling Farrier in Ehrich's custody.

"The wooden leg!" Tesla shouted. "Look at his leg. Surely you remember your old commander."

The penny dropped for a couple of the men. Ehrich could hear them holler "Farrier!" to the others.

Marty Chan

The name seemed to spread like wildfire through the small crowd. The battle still waged beyond. A scrawny hunter retreated, pushing through the crowd and calling, "Commander! Commander. You have to see this."

Ehrich called to the rest of the group. "We're not fighting against you. We're fighting with you."

The hunters lowered their weapons and spoke heatedly amongst themselves. There seemed to be some disagreement as to how to proceed. A few kept their rifles raised, but others hesitated.

Ehrich shoved Farrier ahead and yelled, "We have him as a prisoner. We can turn him over to you and you can do whatever you want with him. Hang him or electrocute him. I don't care which."

Tesla grimaced. "Not electrocute. Anything but that."

Ehrich nodded at Tesla and escorted Farrier one step forward.

Farrier began to push back, his good foot digging into the dirt as he tried to move back. "You can't do this to me, Weisz," he hissed.

"You showed your hand, Farrier. Now pay the price. I'm sure the hunters would love to get their hands on you now that they know you're responsible for the deaths of so many of their squad mates."

"I'll make you a deal," he whispered. "I'll tell you what you need to know if you let me go."

"Not interested. You could be lying to me just like you betrayed the people of this world."

"I betrayed no one. The south should never bow down to the likes of these smug northerners. The country belongs to us."

"You did this to settle the score of the Civil War?" Tesla asked.

"Once a Reb, always a Reb."

"Well, grey coat, it doesn't matter now," Ehrich said. "You're going to face an execution squad for betraying not just the country, but the human race."

He motioned the armed hunters to come closer. Farrier stiffened.

"You want to know where Ba Tian and Kifo are? I'm the only one who can tell you. Turn me over to the hunters and you'll throw away your only chance of stopping the warlord."

"At least I'll have the satisfaction of knowing you'll pay for what you've done to this world."

"I'll tell you everything," Farrier squealed. "Just don't hand me over to them."

"Talk. You'd better hurry."

The hunters drew nearer.

"Ba Tian planned to attack this site and rescue his generals, but Kifo showed up in a new body and with a new plan. He wanted us to split the forces. Kifo knew Edison's men would be spread out between Devil's Island and here. He believed most of the protection would be around the generals."

Ehrich glanced at the remaining hunters on the battlefield and realized the truth in the strategy.

"Where are Kifo and Ba Tian?" Tesla asked.

"This was their best chance to storm Devil's Island and take control of the place. Ba Tian and Kifo are leading my men to Devil's Island. We'll be able to take over the island and hold it for weeks. Long enough for Ba Tian to open the portal and bring through his army. You're all doomed."

Ehrich shot a look at Tesla, his eyes wide with dread. They had been led to think that the generals mattered. He didn't count on Kifo's convincing Ba Tian to focus on the portal. Kifo had outsmarted them all.

"Now will you let me go?" Farrier begged.

"Well, well, well. What do we have here?" a voice boomed.

Ehrich glanced over at Thomas Edison pushing past the crowd, following the scrawny hunter who had run off earlier. The battle waged on in the distance, but the wizened commander was keen on Ehrich and Tesla.

"Mr. Tesla. Is that really you? Why am I not surprised to see you involved with this mess."

Ehrich waved at the old man. "We are on the same side, Mr. Edison. The true enemy is right here."

Farrier glared at Ehrich. "You lied to me."

"I don't know how I'll be able to sleep at night," Ehrich shot back.

Edison stopped in front of the trio. "Is this George Farrier?" he asked the scrawny hunter.

He nodded as did many of the others.

"Well, then. This is a troubling development. A former Demon Watch commander has turned out to be the traitor and Mr. Tesla and Ehrich Weisz have apprehended him. Only they did it with the help of the demons." He glared at the travellers just behind Ehrich and Tesla.

"Travellers or Dimensionals," Ehrich corrected him. "They prefer either of those terms over what you call them."

"I don't actually care about what to call them. I want them out of my dimension."

"But you're targeting the wrong ones. These people mean no harm to anyone. In fact, they've sacrificed their lives and friends to come here to help you."

"Help us with what?"

"The men you are about to execute are generals of an invading force," Tesla explained. "One that has destroyed other worlds and driven refugees to our dimension. The man leading this force intends to do the same to this world. In fact, he's launching an attack on Devil's Island as we stand here."

"A likely story," Edison said.

"Think about it," Ehrich said. "You have in your custody the generals who masterminded the attack on the airship. Why would they want to take over the ship unless it was part of a greater plan? Open your eyes. The machines that are attacking you now are part of a larger force that is about to descend on New York. My people are trying to make sure that doesn't happen. You can fight with us or against us. Either way, we're not going to stop until the forces are put down."

An explosion just beyond the group rocked the area. Edison and the others turned to see the dozen exoskeletons behind the stage engaged in combat with Amina's forces. It was clear from the few travellers left standing that the exoskeletons were winning. The time for discussion was done. Now it was time to pick sides.

Ehrich ordered his fighters, "We have to take the heat off Amina and Hexacate's forces."

The remaining travellers sprang into action, leaving Ehrich alone with Farrier. He stepped back and let two hunters take Farrier into custody. The man limped along, resisting.

"Are you with us, Mr. Edison?" Ehrich asked.

Edison flashed a grim smile. "The enemy of my enemy is my ally."

"What about Farrier?" Tesla asked. "Do you have a place to lock him up?"

"No point in having a traitor in our midst," Edison said. "Chain him to the wagon's wheel. He'll make a good shield if the exoskeletons turn on us."

"No. Wait. Don't!" Farrier pleaded.

Two hunters hauled the one-legged man away while Ehrich and Tesla led the travellers and hunters to fight the enemy.

THE BATTLE TURNS

Ehrich tried to direct the hunters to fire on the left flank, noting that his people were trying to steal behind the lumbering units, but no hunter was willing to take orders from him. Tesla grabbed Ehrich's arm and pulled him down as a volley of disks flew overhead. The melee was chaotic and some of the fighters fell. The travellers tried in vain to sneak behind the units, but the exoskeleton pilots fired on them, pinning them down.

The exoskeletons continued to advance on Thomas Edison's position. Ehrich pulled out his communicator and tried to contact Charlie. "What happened to Amina and Hexacate?"

He waited for a few seconds. Then repeated his call.

Charlie responded. "Dash sees them. Both machines are down. Dash, do you see Amina? Is she all right?"

The communicator hissed for a few seconds, but it seemed like an eternity.

Finally, Charlie clicked back on. "Dash says she's out of the cockpit. No sign of Hexacate. She must still be inside. They're pinned down."

Ehrich clicked off. "We have to move on the exoskeletons before it's too late."

The lanky scientist surveyed the battlefield then the generators near them. "I have an idea."

Ehrich raised an eyebrow in question.

Tesla pointed at the cables snaking across the ground and the giant coils. "I tinkered a bit with the generators earlier so they wouldn't function, but with a few adjustments, I think I can weaponize them."

"Mr. Tesla, do you think you could hurry?"

His friend smiled. "It won't take long. Grab the cables connected to the generators and head to the machines."

He pointed at two long cables coiled beside the generator.

Ehrich turned to two hunters and explained, "We have a way to defeat the units but I need your help. Take these and unroll them."

The hunters turned to each other, unsure whether to obey.

In frustration, he grabbed one by the front of the shirt and screamed into her face. "You either help us or those things cut my friends into ribbons."

This seemed to light a fire under everyone. They dropped their rifles and each uncoiled the cables, snaking them out toward the attacking exoskeletons. The other hunters and travellers advanced on the machines. Smoke filled the air from the downed units.

Ehrich glanced over at his friend, who was now working at the generators. Suddenly, an exoskeleton lumbered through the wreckage in front of the stage and charged toward the generators. Ehrich fired on it with a dynatron pistol. No effect. One of the iron giants raised its arm and fired on the hunters, cutting one of them down. The other dropped the cable and ran for cover.

Ehrich had to stop the attack. He fired on the cockpit. None of the electro darts penetrated, but they did attract the attention of the pilot, who turned the machine around to face Ehrich. He dove to the ground as a volley of disks sliced the air over his head.

The unit continued to advance on the generator. Ehrich stood up and fired, but his pistol cartridge had been spent.

Tesla screamed, "The cable! Grab the cable!"

Ehrich ran to one of the snaking cables and tried to pick up the end. A stray disk slashed at the back of his leg. He tumbled to the ground, clutching his thigh. He rolled upright, holding the end of the cable in one hand. He was a sitting duck. The exoskeleton raised its gun turret and took aim. He braced for his final moment.

A loud hum filled the air and Ehrich's hair stood on end. Then a blinding flash and a loud screech deafened him.

"Point the cable at the unit!" Tesla barked.

Ehrich obeyed. Lightning flew out of the end of the cable and lit up the exoskeleton from top to bottom as the electric current coursed through it. Inside the cockpit, the pilot howled and writhed in pain. Whatever current was electrifying the unit was making its way through the iron and electrocuting the pilot. A second later, the unit went inert, lowering its arms. In the cockpit, the smoking body of the pilot slumped forward.

Tesla ran to pick up the other cable and charged at the dozen units about to decimate Amina's forces. He planted his feet and took aim. Lightning danced out of the cable and lit up the rear units. Ehrich took his cue and followed suit with his cable. The air was singed and the stench of fire filled his nostrils. The two units at the rear toppled over, sizzling with electricity.

The travellers and hunters approaching the units turned around, gaping with wonder. They stopped.

Tesla beamed as he waved them off. The end of his cable was still smoking.

"You weren't kidding when you said you had a powerful weapon, sir," Ehrich said.

Tesla beamed. "It's like a cannon. The cable is the conduit. You just have to aim and shoot."

"What's the range on this?" Ehrich asked.

"About fifty feet, but the cable is long, so you'll be able to get closer to the battle. Let's finish this, shall we?"

They charged at the units attacking Amina's forces. Ehrich aimed at the nearest unit. Beside him, Tesla followed suit. Two bursts of pure white electrical energy shot out from the cables and caught two of the units. They stopped moving immediately.

The travellers cheered and fired upon the remaining units, which began to turn to engage. The hunters fired on the attackers. Fire sparked on two of the units and the exoskeletons seized up. The tide was turning. Ehrich cheered as he hauled his cable across the field and launched another bolt of energy at an exoskeleton now trying to flee the battlefield.

The unit lurched to a halt and the humans cheered. Ehrich barked at them, "Get into the unit. Pull out the pilot. You can use the machines against them."

Edison yelled, "You heard him. Get inside!"

Four hunters rushed to the inert exoskeleton. Two provided cover fire on the other machines, using the iron behemoth as protection against the flying disks. With the Tesla cannon, they were able to turn the tide of battle. The hunters and travellers engaged the remaining exoskeletons, moving further away from the stage and the paddy wagons.

Ehrich dropped his cable and rushed to his friends' fallen units. Amina peeked up from the other side of one of the exoskeletons, propping up Hexacate and her son as they rose from the wreckage.

"Amina!" he yelled.

She waved. "We're safe."

Ehrich stopped in front of her and checked her for wounds. She seemed none the worse for wear. Then he checked on Hexacate and her son.

"We're sturdier than we look," Hexacate said.

"Took you long enough," Amina quipped.

"Sorry, I had to stop and sightsee."

"Well, I see Mr. Tesla found a new toy to play with. Impressive electricity cannon."

"I wish the generators were portable. We could use this for what's to come."

She cocked her head to one side, confused. Before he could explain, Edison and Tesla joined the group along with some of the surviving hunters and travellers. They stood shoulder to shoulder, humans and Dimensionals as brothers in arms.

Edison eyed the paddy wagons. "We have the generals. Now we need to put an end to the rest of the forces."

Ehrich shook his head. "We have to get to Devil's Island."

"No, we have to finish the battle here."

"You do, but we have unfinished business with Ba Tian and Kifo."

An explosion from the battlefield interrupted their argument. The battle wasn't over yet.

Edison turned from Ehrich and ordered, "Give them help. Go. Go!"

Both the hunters and travellers trotted off to the battlefield with Edison urging them on.

DIVERSION

Ehrich pulled out his communicator and signalled Charlie, Dash, and Bess. "Do you read me? We are all safe, but the battle is still going on. Stay where you are. I'll let you know what we're doing next."

Charlie answered. "Looks like the hunters and travellers are working together. Is that what I'm seeing?"

Ehrich replied. "Yes. For now. How are Dash and Bess?"

"Your brother has eagle eyes, but he's got no stamina. Bess has been doing all the pushing."

Over the communicator, Ehrich could hear Bess's voice. "You could stand to lose some weight, Charlie."

Amina scratched her head. "I thought there would be more exoskeletons. I swear there were far more taken from the tunnel."

"There were," Ehrich said. "This was a diversion attack. The real plan was to take over the Demon Gate portal on Devil's Island. Ba Tian wanted Edison to concentrate the hunters on the execution site so that the island wouldn't be well defended."

"How do you know?"

"We captured Farrier," he said. "He told us everything."

"If Ba Tian secures the portal, there will be no stopping his army. We have to get to the island."

The others agreed, but Tesla pointed out, "We can't take the exoskeletons with us. They'll slow us down."

Amina nodded. "We can't waste time. Leave them."

"What's the fastest way to the Island?" Hexacate asked.

"The train is out. We can't return to Manhattan. We'd have to sail up the East River."

Dash beamed. "I know where there are boats."

Gur-Rahim perked up. "And my mom is the best sailor I know."

"Would you help us, Hexacate?" Ehrich asked.

"I hate the thought of having to relocate to a new dimension."

"Then let's go to the boathouse."

—\/\/\/—

Ehrich sprinted to the nearest boathouse as Amina and the others followed suit. Along the way, Ehrich signalled Charlie, Dash, and Bess to meet him at the pier. When they reached the boathouse, Hexacate and a small group of her travellers prepped three boats for take-off. She swung the boom around, checked the sail, and helped tighten the ropes on the main boat.

Ehrich stood outside watching for his friends and Dash. When he spotted them, Bess was struggling to push the wheelchair through the sand while Dash walked ahead of them. Ehrich ran to help her.

"I'll take over," Ehrich said. He gripped the handles on the back of the chair and pushed. The chair dug into the sand.

"Dash, give us a hand," Ehrich said.

His brother trudged behind the chair.

"Let's do it together," Bess said, taking one of the other handles.

As the trio pushed Charlie to the boathouse, Bess eyed Ehrich. "You don't look any worse for wear. Battle seems to suit you."

He grinned. "I would rather make coins disappear than this."

"Well, you weren't very good at that. I could always see your windows."

He feigned disgust. "I kept my fingers tight."

"Not tight enough. You always flashed the coin through these two fingers." She held up her first and middle fingers, parting them slightly to show Ehrich the mistake he had made.

"Well, that's because you know what you're looking for."

"Either that or you're a terrible magician."

Dash quipped. "He's a terrible magician."

"You think you can do better, Bess?" Ehrich asked.

"Without a doubt."

Charlie covered his ears and groaned. "Enough. Enough already. Why don't you just kiss and get it over with?"

Ehrich and Bess gasped, "What?"

"The way you two go on, it's obvious there's something between you. Ehrich, you haven't taken your eyes off Bess since you found her. And Bess, you've talked about him until my ears nearly bled. Just admit you like each other."

"I do not," Bess said.

"You don't?" Ehrich said, before catching himself. "I mean, I don't ... It's not ... Well ..."

Dash laughed. "Ehrich likes Bess. Ehrich likes Bess."

"What ... no ... I mean ..."

Charlie laughed. "Easy there, smooth talker. I'm not judging you. I'm just saying life's too short to play coy."

Ehrich and Bess said nothing more. When they arrived at the boathouse, Amina and Tesla rushed out to help them. Charlie's condition was going to be a problem if they had to move quickly on the island.

Amina shot a look at Ehrich. He mouthed, "I know."

Bess struggled to push the chair through the narrow doorway of the boathouse while Dash directed the chair forward.

"Charlie, I'm sorry about this, but we need stealth on the island," Ehrich said. "You're going to have to sit this one out."

"There is no blasted way you're keeping me out of this fight. Now that I have the taste for battle again, I want more. I can help you. Maybe not with the actual fighting, but I can report positions and advantages to you." He held up the communicator.

"On the island, we'll have to move fast to get to Demon Gate. I don't want you to slow us down."

"I'll be the best help you'll ever have. The hunters aren't just going to let you waltz down to Demon Gate. They know me. I can lead you down there. They see you, they're going to clap you in irons."

Tesla nodded. "We are still on their wanted list, Ehrich. The boy does have a point."

"But we can barely get him in the boat."

Bess put her foot down. "We're running out of time arguing. Either load him in the boat or don't, but this talk isn't doing any of us any good."

Ehrich relented and loaded Charlie and his wheelchair onto the boat. They pushed off and set sail. Hexacate steered the tiller, turning the boat into the choppy water. She unfurled the sail as they left the boathouse and angled it to catch a strong wind. The boat surged ahead, rocking up and down as it skirted the ocean waves. Behind them, the other travellers manned the two smaller boats and kept pace.

•—⋀⋁⋀—•

A half-hour later, they were heading around the bend of Coney Island and toward the mouth of the East River. As the boat travelled up the river, Ehrich made his way to the prow and clung to the gunwale. The choppy waters threatened to buck the boat over at any time, but Hexacate didn't seem to be panicked. Ehrich took this as a good sign as he scanned the horizon ahead.

Bess slid in beside him and crossed her arms over her chest against the biting wind. He offered her his jacket but she waved him off. "I'm fine. The cold air is keeping me alert."

"You don't have to be part of this battle, Bess. We could drop you off at any point."

"I've committed myself. I can't back away now."

"Yes, but you've done more than enough for us."

"Don't be patronizing, Ehrich. You've kept me out of harm's way for most of this, and I should remind you that I can take care of myself."

He smiled. "Yes, I don't doubt that for a minute. I don't want to take any more chances."

"Listen to me, Ehrich. Protecting me like I'm some delicate flower is the surest way to lose me."

"I'm sorry. It's just that since I lost Dash to Kifo, I've been overcautious with the people I care about."

She stopped for a minute. "You care about me?"

Silence. He hadn't expected to talk to Bess about his feelings right before launching into the final battle, but now he found himself sinking in the mire of a serious discussion, and he wasn't even sure how he felt himself. The only thing he knew for sure was that he wanted to be with Bess, but he was torn.

The only way to be with her was to remain in this dimension, and he had already promised Dash that he would get his brother home. With all that Dash had suffered, Ehrich couldn't even consider asking the boy to give up more. He needed to return Dash home to their own world and their parents. In order to do that, Ehrich would have to put his brother ahead of Bess, and he wasn't able to bring himself to admit that just yet.

Suddenly, a hard punch to his arm shook him out of his thoughts. "You're not slipping away that easily, Ehrich. I care about you as well, but I'm not about to shove you behind me so I can protect you. I don't need a knight. I need to help."

"Ow, you pack a mean punch."

"Don't you forget it. I can add a lot to this team if you stop seeing me as a girl and start seeing me the way you see Amina."

Ehrich cut short a laugh. "You know that Amina is a girl."

She shook her head. "That's not the point. I mean you treat her more like an equal. A warrior. You're not afraid when she goes into battle. It's like you trust her to take care of herself, but you don't trust me."

"She's seen more fights than either of us combined, Bess. She's used to this."

"I might not have seen as many fights, but I know how to keep my eyes open. If I get into anything I can't handle, I can back off. I don't need you to be looking over my shoulder or getting distracted from what you're doing because you think I need to be rescued."

"I'm sorry, Bess. I didn't realize that's how I've been treating you. What can I do?"

"You can stop worrying about me like a dog looking out for its master. You need to focus. I'm not about to be the reason you lose this war."

He slowly nodded. "I've got to keep my head on straight."

"Exactly."

To that end, Ehrich turned his attention to the river and Devil's Island in the distance. At first he thought a thunderstorm was blowing into New York. Flashes lit up the sky, but they were low on the horizon. He turned back to Tesla. "Sir, does that look like a storm to you?"

Tesla craned his neck to get a better view. He shook his head. "That's not a storm. That's a firefight."

Charlie nodded. "Yes, I'd recognize Teslatron fire anywhere. Looks like Ba Tian's forces have reached the island."

Ehrich yelled back at Hexacate and her son. "Is there any way you can get us there faster?"

She shook her head. "I can only go as fast as the wind can carry us."

"Then we had better hope the hunters can hold off the exoskeletons," Ehrich said.

He gripped the sides of the boat and gritted his teeth. He had hoped Edison's fighters might be able to defend the island against the exoskeletons. As long as he could see flashes of light, it meant the hunters were still fighting. Maybe it was his imagination, but the flashes seemed to dwindle.

Finally, the boat landed on Devil's Island. Ehrich hopped out first. He could see the extent of the damage. Ba Tian's exoskeleton forces seemed to have been split between the main compound and the hunter barracks. There were more machines here than on Coney Island. Ehrich counted at least 60 units spread across the field. The bulk of the hunter defenses had fallen back to the compound. Most of the exoskeletons were marching on the compound while twenty split off to the right to engage a smaller group of hunters trying to defend the barracks.

The others joined Ehrich and surveyed the battlefield. He turned to Amina. "What do you think?"

"Demon Gate is his goal, but his forces are too strong for us to take down with these handheld weapons. We'd be better off taking down the exoskeletons at the barracks and using them to attack the other forces."

Bess shook her head. "We'd still be outnumbered."

Tesla pointed out, "It seems to me that we don't need to defeat the exoskeleton machines out here. They are too large to get into the lower depths of Demon Gate. Ba Tian will have to leave behind the exoskeletons. We just need to go down there before he and his forces do."

Amina agreed, "We need to find a way to keep most of his units occupied up here."

"There are too many of them," Dash pointed out.

"Then we go with Amina's idea. Take control of the units attacking the barracks," Bess said. "Misdirection."

Ehrich beamed. "Yes. If we can convince the hunters we're on their side, we might have the distraction we need."

CHARLIE'S DAY

The group moved on the exoskeletons at the barracks. The two-storey building lit up with lights as hunters took positions at the windows and fired down on the exoskeletons. The twenty units were advancing on the building, forcing back the ten hunters who defended the front entrance. Ehrich directed Hexacate and her travellers to sneak behind the exoskeletons. He signalled the coordinated attack.

One striker yanked open the hatch while the other fired into the cockpit, knocking out the pilot. They repeated this ploy six times, securing half a dozen of the units.

Ehrich climbed into his unit and hauled his brother up to join him. He closed the hatch, then operated the controls to aim the weapon turret at the servo of the unit in front of him. He waited until the others were in position. Then he raised the machine arm and signalled for everyone to fire at their targets. Five explosions rocked the area as the next row of exoskeletons went down. Ehrich then adjusted the aim and fired upon the next unit. They'd have enough time to take down at least another three or four units before the rest turned around.

He hit his mark as did Bess and Amina. The others missed, leaving nine units left to face them. The exoskeletons turned to meet the new enemy. Ehrich and his group used the inert units as cover. He hopped out of his cockpit, leaving Dash to pilot it. Amina and Bess joined him on the ground.

"We need to get behind them," Ehrich said.

"The hunters will fire on us," Amina pointed out.

"Not if Charlie is with us," Bess said.

"She's right. We need Charlie."

They rushed to the edge of the battlefield. Bess led the way while Ehrich and Amina pushed Charlie ahead. Hexacate's forces met head-on with the remaining exoskeletons. Farrier's men were too busy concentrating their fire on the attacking exoskeletons to notice Ehrich and his group slip past.

Charlie ordered, "I need one of you to get me to the hunters."

"I'll do it," Bess said. "You two are probably still on the most wanted list."

Ehrich cracked a smile and grabbed Amina. They headed to the nearest attacking unit so they could climb into the cockpit. Energy beams lit up the air, forcing them to duck. They had to retreat from the Teslatron rifles firing at them.

Bess wheeled Charlie to the barracks. He waved and screamed, "Cease fire! We're on your side. Hold your fire!"

Two fighters took aim at Charlie and Bess, but a third one signalled them to lower their weapons. It was Elizabeth, one of the hunters who had visited Charlie at the home. "What in tarnation are you doing here?"

"Long story, but the short version is we're here to help you take down those machines. Watch and learn."

Now that the hunters had stopped firing, Ehrich and Amina sprinted to the unit. He pulled open the hatch and she fired inside. The unit went inert.

Charlie yelled, "Elizabeth, their weak spot is underneath the unit, but you can also take them down if you fire into the servo pack on their backs, but the pistols and rifles aren't going to do the damage. The real impact is if you take the reins of these big bad giants and let loose."

The hunters gathered around Charlie but Bess was impatient. "Better to show than to tell." She hopped up into the cockpit and closed the hatch.

The machine swivelled around and took aim at the nearest unit. Bess gripped the toggle on the handle and fired into the back of the unit, igniting sparks and rendering the iron giant inert like so many of the others in the metal graveyard. She advanced on the next unit and repeated the action.

Below, Charlie directed the hunters to split up the other units and steal under them as Ehrich and Amina had done. They were quick to pick up on the trick and were able to incapacitate the pilots in the remaining units of the attack force.

Ehrich beamed at the successful raid as he waved Dash and Bess over. The younger Weisz climbed out of his cockpit and waited for Bess to come out of hers. Together, they jogged over and joined the others. As soon as the hunters saw the travellers, they raised their weapons.

Charlie wheeled over to them and waved his arms frantically. "No, no. They're on our side. They're all with me."

"What are you doing with Dimensionals?" one fighter asked.

"They are here to help fight the invaders. You want to arrest the only people who can help you save Devil's Island? Go ahead. I aim to keep the island from falling into enemy hands. You with me or against me?"

He didn't wait for an answer. He wheeled to the nearest operational unit and lifted his arm. Hexacate rushed over to help lift Charlie into the unit. He peeked out. "I can't work the pedals. Who's coming in to help me?"

The hunters glanced at each other. One slowly raised her hand and jogged over to climb into the unit. Ehrich and his companions directed the others into the remaining functional units and taught them the basics of the controls. Hexacate and her forces then returned to their units to prepare for the final attack.

Ehrich, Amina, Tesla, Bess, and Dash remained on the ground. Ehrich explained to the others, "We have to get down to Demon Gate and stop Ba Tian from using the portal. If we can get there before him, I might be able to destroy the controls. If he's there, we might have to fight."

Tesla picked up one of the rifles and eyed it. "I think I have a way to destroy the machinery. I can turn this into a bomb."

Amina nodded. "Good idea. Let's blow up the gate and make sure that Ba Tian never has a chance to use it."

Dash argued, "But isn't that our only way home?"

Ehrich hesitated. "I'm sure we can find another way back."

"You promised you'd take me home."

Ehrich glanced at the others, searching for an answer. "Dash, if there's a way we can stop Ba Tian without destroying the portal, we'll do it, but we need this bomb as a last resort."

"Are you sure you want to go back home?"

"Why would you think that?"

Dash mumbled, "I saw you with Bess. You like her. I can see that. Everyone can see that."

"I made a promise, Dash, and I will keep it. Trust me."

Dash nodded.

Ehrich turned to the others. "Let's get down there first and see what the situation is. I haven't seen Ba Tian, Kifo, or Ole Lukoje among the exoskeletons, so maybe they're directing the battle from the shore."

The group made their way along the edge of the battle to the headquarters building. The fighting was fierce between the hunters and the larger force of exoskeletons. Charlie led his force of exoskeletons to attack from behind. Though they had smaller numbers, they had the element of surprise. A dozen units fell within the first attack, but the others swivelled around to match up against their counterparts. All Charlie had to do was distract the main forces long enough for Ehrich and his allies to slip past them.

Rather than use the front entrance, Ehrich edged up to one of the office windows and smashed it open. There was no time for stealth. By this point, every hunter on the island was either engaged in battle or dying. He cleared away the glass then lifted Amina into the building. Tesla followed, then Bess. Ehrich hoisted his little brother inside and climbed in after the group.

They navigated through the hallways with Tesla leading the way. They reached an intersection and Tesla veered to the right. Stairs were straight ahead. This was the way down to Demon Gate. At the very least, they had the advantage of knowing the layout of the headquarters while Ba Tian and his forces were travelling without a map. Ehrich considered the possibility that Farrier might have instructed them how to descend to the lower levels, but even with instructions, it would be easy to get lost in the maze of corridors.

He took the lead and headed down the steps with his weapons at the ready. The rest of the group stayed a single flight of stairs behind him. When Ehrich signalled the coast was clear, they descended.

They made their way down to the next level and eventually reached the lowest level. Ahead was the corridor that would eventually lead to Demon Gate. They were halfway down the hallway when a figure emerged from around the corner. It was Kifo in Mr. Serenity's body. Two soldiers stepped in line behind him to block off the passageway. Ba Tian had beaten them down to the portal.

"I know another way to the portal," Tesla said.

"We have to deal with them first," Amina replied.

"No time," Ehrich said. "If Ba Tian is down here, he'll be opening the portal to let in the rest of his soldiers. We can't fight them."

"Kifo!" Dash growled. "He's the reason for all of this."

Ehrich grabbed his brother by the arm. "Dash. Focus. We have another mission. We have to get home."

Amina barked, "Go! I'll hold them off."

"On your own?" Bess asked.

"I can handle them."

Ehrich nodded at his friend and led the group back down the hallway to find the other route to Demon Gate. He was about to round the corner when a shout caught his attention. Amina was yelling at Dash to join the others.

"Kifo!" Dash yelled.

Ehrich started after his brother, but the firefight in the hallway erupted. Energy bolts sizzled through the air. He couldn't reach them without being hit.

Tesla pulled at his arm. "We have to stop Ba Tian."

Ehrich hesitated, unsure which way to go. Bess grabbed his hand. "Your brother will be okay. Amina will protect him."

He reluctantly nodded and turned to join the others. He took one last glance back at the fight in the hallway. Amina and Dash were on their own.

He hated leaving his brother, but he had to get to Demon Gate. He led the group away.

KIFO

Amina pulled Dash back around the corner as the air sizzled from a Teslatron blast. She lowered herself and swung the rifle around the corner to return fire. A scream. She guessed she had scored a hit. Dash grabbed the pistol from her belt and took aim down the hall, firing two darts before she pulled him back. An energy blast seared the wall where he had been standing a second earlier.

"Kifo has to pay for what he did," Dash said.

"Yes, but if you get hurt, your brother is going to kill me."

He shook his head. "I owe him."

"Don't even think about it, Dash."

Too late. The young Weisz sprinted across the open hallway as the air sizzled with electricity. Amina had to act fast. She swung around the corner as an energy bolt seared the opposite wall. One of Farrier's soldiers was firing at Dash. Just behind him, Kifo was reaching down to pick up the fallen weapon from an unconscious soldier on the ground.

Farrier's soldier took aim at Dash who raised his pistol and pulled the trigger. Nothing came out. The gun was jammed. Dash was defenseless.

"Duck!" Amina cried out.

He did, just as she fired her rifle into the chest of the soldier. The man convulsed and staggered back into Kifo, knocking the weapon out of his hands. She took aim at Kifo, but though she knew her mentor Mr. Serenity was now possessed, she couldn't bring herself to fire on him.

Kifo shook off the soldier and turned to face Amina. She trained the weapon on him.

Dash shouted, "Shoot him! Amina! Shoot!"

She hesitated.

"You know there is a chance to save your precious Mr. Serenity," Kifo taunted. "But not if you shoot me."

She aimed the rifle, but she couldn't bring herself to do it. Kifo advanced a few more steps.

"What are you waiting for, Amina?! Shoot him!"

"I can't. He's still Mr. Serenity in my eyes." She lowered her rifle.

Kifo took another step forward. "Yes, he's here still." He lifted the Infinity Coil from under his shirt. "And if you ever want to see him again, you'll drop your weapon."

Dash let out a war whoop and charged at Kifo. The beefy man swatted the boy away, slamming him into the wall. Dash slumped to the ground, stunned.

This spurred Amina to action. She raised her rifle to fire, but Kifo lunged at her. His hands reached for her throat. She kicked him in the gut, forcing him to back away. She turned her body but he was quicker. He wrapped an arm around her neck. She tried to throw him off, but the man had leverage and wasn't about to let go. She kicked backward, but struck only air. She reached behind her head and tried to box his ears. No effect. She grabbed a part of his shirt and pulled but he maintained a firm grip. She thought she heard a snap and wondered if it was one of her tendons. Pain shot through her throat as he squeezed harder.

"Drop the weapon," he hissed in her ear.

She began to feel lightheaded. The rifle clattered to the stone floor. He increased the pressure against her throat. The light began to fade before her eyes. She couldn't catch her next breath.

Out of the corner of her eye, she spotted Dash bending over to pick up the Teslatron.

Kifo laughed. "Little man, you're going to shoot me? Careful, you might hit your companion."

Dash straightened up but not with the rifle. Instead, he held in his hand the Infinity Coil, which dangled from a broken cord.

Kifo growled. "Give that back to me." He loosened his grip around Amina's throat.

Dash shook his head. "Never." He picked up the Teslatron. "I'm going to make sure you never get to use it again."

"Don't even consider it, or your friend will perish." Kifo squeezed, causing Amina to gag and struggle.

"You know what will happen if I unload all the energy into the Infinity Coil, don't you?" Dash asked.

"Nothing. It won't do a thing."

Dash tapped his head. "I've shared your consciousness, Kifo. I know when you're afraid. I can sense it right now."

"Hardly."

"Then let's find out." He tossed the medallion on the floor and took aim with the rifle.

"Wait!" Kifo shouted. "You destroy the coil and you will doom all the souls within. Your friend Mr. Serenity, Ning Shu, all of them. The ones who supported you in the void. You will be sentencing them to death. When the amulet is destroyed, all the souls will be untethered and cast adrift in the universe."

"At least they will be released. They were dead as soon as you took over their bodies and left the shells behind."

Amina pushed back again, but Kifo exerted more force with his chokehold. She started to see spots and knew that she was going to pass out soon. She tried to conserve her breath. Kifo angled himself to get closer to Dash, but Amina pushed against him and kept him at bay.

Dash kept the rifle aimed at the amulet. "I will put an end to you, Kifo. You'd be trapped in one body and when it dies, you die with it."

"You will be responsible for the death of thousands of souls. Can you live with that?"

Dash hesitated for a second.

"Back away from the amulet and I will let her go."

Amina gasped for air and steeled herself for the end. She tried to speak, but the pressure on her throat had reduced her voice to a croak. "Destroy it."

Dash wasn't sure what she had said, but he knew he couldn't let her die, even if it meant that Kifo would regain the amulet. Then an idea sprang into his mind. All the time he had spent in the void of the Infinity Coil, he had felt the presence of others, and the shift from dread and hopelessness to tangible fear when Kifo added another soul to the prison. He recalled how the universe seemed to unfold and open up to bring through the falling soul. He wondered if he could open that universe now. He knew it would come at a price, but he had to try.

"Hold on, Kifo. You win."

"Back away from the Infinity Coil."

Instead, Dash bent over and picked up the amulet and held it in his hand. The metal felt hot to his skin and he noted the never-ending gears whirring and ticking within the heart of the mechanism. He began to walk to Kifo with the amulet held out. He dropped the rifle at his feet.

Kifo cracked a grin. He kept Amina in front of him, but he shifted himself so he could reach out with his free hand to take the amulet being offered. He hesitated when he smelled sulphur. "What do you think you're doing? Stop it."

But Dash wasn't listening. He closed his eyes and concentrated, willing the Infinity Coil in his hand to open up the universe as he had seen from the other side. The gears ticked loudly in his ears and he could feel the metal grow warmer to the touch, to the point where he almost wanted to drop it. He clutched the amulet harder and gritted his teeth as he heard the voices of a thousand souls shout out in unison.

Smoke poured from the Infinity Coil. Kifo relaxed his grip. Amina elbowed him in the side and pulled away. The man staggered backward, holding up his hands against the smoke that writhed in the air like a cobra and moved closer to him. Amina stepped aside, but the smoke seemed to have a mind of its own, curling around and past her and making a path straight to Kifo. The rotund man backed away.

Dash thrust the Infinity Coil in front of him and aimed it right at Kifo. More smoke poured out and engulfed Kifo in a cloud. The assassin let out a scream, but it was drowned out by the sound of a thousand voices calling out.

Amina scrambled away, moving behind Dash and picking up the fallen Teslatron. When she looked up again, the sulphur smell was almost unbearable. The smoke was pouring into the eyes and mouth of Kifo as he thrashed about. Dash continued to press forward.

There was silence for a moment as Kifo froze, then the smoke began to pour out of his eyes and mouth and head toward Dash. The boy began to back up, but the smoke was coming for him like a snake after its prey. Amina guessed this was how Kifo had taken over the bodies of his victims. The smoke would enter the Infinity Coil and disappear into the void.

Slowly, smoke began to emerge from the backside of the coil and the black tendrils reached out to Dash. The boy was oblivious, with his eyes closed. Amina acted quickly, knocking the Infinity Coil out of Dash's hand. It clattered to the ground as the black smoke poured back into it and wisps of smoke emerged to reach out to Dash.

Amina took aim with the Teslatron rifle and fired into the device. Over and over again. The amulet absorbed the energy as the smoke continued to pour in and seep out. She fired twice more and then, suddenly, a brilliant flash erupted from the centre of the Infinity Coil.

A hurricane-force wind blew Amina against the wall. The deafening roar of a thousand voices filled the corridor. The smoke recoiled, rushing back into the Infinity Coil then dispersing as the voices faded.

Then all was silent. The amulet was shattered into pieces. Dash was prone on the floor. Beside him, the unconscious form of Kifo in Mr. Serenity's body. Amina rushed to Dash's side and tried to revive him.

"Dash. Dash? Dash." She slapped his face until his eyelids fluttered.

He opened his eyes. "Amina. What happened?"

"I destroyed the Infinity Coil."

"Where is Kifo?"

She looked around, unsure. "He might still be in Mr. Serenity's body."

Dash shook his head. "I don't think that's the way the Infinity Coil works. The smoke is the soul. That's how he transfers into the bodies."

"But now that the amulet is destroyed, what happens to the souls?"

Dash looked down at the broken device. "I'm afraid that was the only thing that kept them alive."

"They're all gone?"

He closed his eyes for a moment. "They are no longer trapped."

A low groan came from a few feet away. Amina grabbed the rifle and swung around. Mr. Serenity was stirring on the floor. She took aim and pushed Dash behind her, worried Kifo still had possession of her mentor.

"Oh, my aching everything."

"Mr. Serenity?" Amina called out.

The rotund man looked around the corridor. "Where am I?"

"Do you think it's really him, Dash?"

The young Weisz nodded. "I felt Kifo's presence in the Infinity Coil just before you destroyed it."

"But how did Mr. Serenity get out?"

"I imagine the same way I did. If the host body still exists, the consciousness will try to reconnect with it."

"And what about Kifo?"

"I think his original body is dust by now. He's like the other souls that were trapped. Adrift."

Amina headed over to Mr. Serenity and took hold of his arm to help him up. "You're safe, Mr. Serenity. We're on Devil's Island."

Mr. Serenity squinted at his ward. "Amina, your idea of safe is very different from mine."

She smiled and hugged him.

Dash pulled on her sleeve. "We have to help Ehrich."

Her reunion with her mentor would have to wait. She led the way down the hall in the direction Ehrich and the others had gone, hoping she could navigate the maze to Demon Gate.

FINAL BATTLE

Far below the surface, Ehrich led Bess and Tesla to the entrance of the Demon Gate portal. Two of Farrier's soldiers stood outside the doorway. Ehrich primed his rifle as did Bess. They nodded to each other and charged around the corner, firing at the soldiers. The unsuspecting guards went down before they could even draw their weapons. The path to Demon Gate was clear. They moved quickly toward the doors.

The door opened and Ba Tian smiled at the approaching group. "I thought there was a commotion out here. Just the people I wanted to see. I'm sure one of you knows how to operate the equipment to open the portal."

"You won't get the chance to use it." Ehrich raised his rifle to fire, but a metal hand from the doorway next to him slashed the rifle barrel in two, leaving the weapon useless.

Ehrich turned to face his new assailant. Ole Lukoje punched him in the stomach, causing him to double over. Bess swung her rifle around. A sharp disk embedded itself in her hand. She dropped her weapon and glanced up at the source. Ba Tian held a ring of the disks in one hand, ready to flick the throwing stars.

"Now, now, let's not get off on the wrong foot," the crimson warlord clucked. "I think we'll get along swimmingly if you just give me what I want."

Tesla growled. "You have some nerve to demand anything from us."

"Oh, but it's not an order. Think of it as more of a bargain. You open the portal for me, and I will let you return to your world, Ehrich. Isn't that what you always wanted?"

Ehrich cocked his head to one side and stared at Ba Tian, then back at Ole Lukoje. "You're offering me a way home? How do I know you won't just invade that world as soon as I go through?"

Ba Tian smiled. "You have my word of honour. Passing on your world is a small price to pay for the rest of the universe."

Tesla was about to say something but Ehrich shook his head. "No, Mr. Tesla. This is my decision. Show me my world and I'll consider helping you. Open a portal, Ole Lukoje."

The raggedy man reached into his pocket for the nano-dust he needed to open a dimensional portal.

Ehrich stopped him. "Not here. In the Demon Gate chamber." He was taking a chance that the raggedy man had no idea about the dangers of two portals opening in the same location.

Ole Lukoje shrugged. "It matters-s-s not to me where we open my portal."

Ba Tian stepped aside and allowed the group to pass through. Tesla lowered his makeshift bomb to the floor and followed the others.

To one side of the room, the portal area was a bare alcove. Opposite the empty space sat the equipment to operate it. The console with various diodes, gauges, and gears loomed large in Ehrich's eyes. There was one other door in the room, which was the doorway the newly arrived travellers would have to go through for processing. Normally, the hunters stood guard at the console and doors. Without their presence, the large room seemed cavernous.

Ole Lukoje set up in the middle of the room. He reached into his pocket and retrieved his dust. He tossed the particles in the air. They shimmered, tearing the fabric of space.

Ehrich recalled the last time he had seen the raggedy man pull off this stunt. They had used the same portal to take out Ba Tian. The warlord must have remembered, too, because he backed away behind the console.

The portal opened like a cat's eye, revealing a myriad of worlds beyond. It was small enough for one or two people to slide through, but hardly large enough for an army. Ole Lukoje narrowed his eyes and waved his hands, slowing the images down until Ehrich recognized the Appleton he had lived in. He saw the graveyard where he had first encountered Kifo, unaware that the assassin had possessed his brother. A lump formed in his stomach and came out of his throat in the form of one word: "Home."

Ba Tian laughed. "And it can all be yours if you return me the favour of opening the portal here in Demon Gate."

Tesla warned, "Don't do it."

"We have no other choice, sir. If we want to put an end to everything, we have to give Ba Tian what he wants."

"You won't be ending anything," Bess said. "You'll just be

getting out of here to leave the rest of us to his forces."

"You can come with Dash and me."

"I can't leave behind the only world I know."

"I'm sorry, Bess, but this is the only way." He shot a look at Tesla, who grimly nodded and walked over to join Ehrich at the console.

Bess started after them, but Ole Lukoje grabbed her by the arm. "No, my dear. You'll s-s-stay with me to guarantee they follow through with what they promis-s-s-e."

Tesla joined Ehrich at the console and began to manipulate the dials. Ba Tian watched carefully, asking questions about the functions of the gears, absorbing all the procedures.

"You must be careful with your selection of the worlds," Tesla explained. "We can narrow down the field to a few worlds. The portal will be stable, but we can only bring a few over at a time. We've never tried to bring in any more than that because the hunters have to process them."

"But you can bring more, can't you?" Ba Tian asked.

Tesla shrugged. "You'll be the first to try. As long as the portal stays open, you can bring through as many as you want."

"Excellent. Open the portal."

Tesla shot a look at Ehrich. Then he proceeded to pull the lever. A screech filled the air as the Demon Gate alcove shimmered and lit up. The raggedy man and Bess were standing between Ehrich and the gate. Ehrich began to inch over, ready to sprint and grab Bess, but Ba Tian caught the movement.

"It's a trap," Ba Tian yelled. He swatted Tesla across the face and knocked the scientist against the wall, but it was too late.

The portal opened fully and the air distorted as the fields of two portals intersected with each other. The worlds shimmered in and out of form as the room itself began to bend out of shape. Ba Tian clung to the console as a powerful wind picked up. The two portals merged into one amoeba-shaped portal that threatened to suck everything inside it. Bess ran from the portal with Ole Lukoje on her heels. She reached the console and grabbed on. He had hold of her legs as the powerful force lifted both of them off the floor. Ehrich braced himself against the console and reached out to Bess.

"Take my hand!" he screamed, but the roaring wind drowned him out.

He felt something slam against the back of his legs. The unconscious Tesla had slid over and pinned one of Ehrich's legs against the console.

Next to him, Ba Tian made his way across the console to shut down the machine. Ehrich had to fend him off and save Bess. He couldn't do both at the same time. Ba Tian had let go of the console as he tried to reach for the control next to Ehrich. This was his only shot.

Ehrich howled as he swung at the crimson warlord and caught him in the jaw. It had little effect on Ba Tian. He grinned at Ehrich, grabbed the boy by the hair and hauled him over. Tesla's body slammed against the bottom of the console as Ehrich's leg pulled free. Ba Tian smashed his head into the console.

When Ehrich lifted his head, he felt a trickle of liquid running from both nostrils. The pain was excruciating, but he couldn't give up. He threw another punch at Ba Tian, but the warlord easily grabbed his fist and began to squeeze.

Ehrich howled in pain, trying to pull himself free. Ba Tian would not relent. He gripped Ehrich's hair harder and prepared to slam his face into the console again. Ehrich placed both hands on the console to keep himself upright, but the man was stronger.

Ba Tian grinned. "I will visit havoc on your world for your betrayal."

The crimson warlord gripped Ehrich's head for one final blow.

—◦‑∿∿‑◦—

At the other end of the console, Bess clung to the edge, screaming in pain as Ole Lukoje's metal claws tore at her legs. He climbed up her body, struggling against the suction of the vortex. The gale force winds threatened to throw both of them into the distortion field.

Bess redoubled her efforts to hang on to the console. The raggedy man's claws now dug into her back. She shrieked.

She began to pull herself further up the console, fighting off the pain of his claws digging into her body. Her arms started to give out.

Suddenly, a metal claw slashed her arm, drawing blood. Ole Lukoje was now face to face with Bess. He was so close. She could smell his fetid breath. He raised his claw to strike a killing blow. His other hand clutched the edge of the console.

Bess had one chance. She slid her hand across and dug her fingernails into his wrist with all her strength. The shock and pain was immediate. Ole Lukoje let go, and the force of the wind sucked him toward the distortion field. He stabbed one metal claw into the floor like a climbing piton. He did the same with the other claw, anchoring himself against the suction of the vortex.

Bess regained her grip on the console, but her strength was starting to ebb. Ole Lukoje howled in terror, his arms flailing. One claw after the other, he began to pull himself back toward Bess. His crooked smile flashed. "Time to die, little pes-s-st."

Ehrich gritted his teeth. The crimson warlord was obviously stronger, but he could turn this to his advantage. He pulled away, feeling some of his hair come out by the roots. He ignored the pain.

Ba Tian clutched the boy's hair tighter and pulled him over. This time, Ehrich did not resist. He pitched his body toward Ba Tian, throwing the man off balance. Ehrich gripped the lever on the panel, then threw his legs up, using the suction of the void to lift him. Both feet connected against Ba Tian's chin, stunning the warlord. He staggered back and the void's vacuum energy drew him away from the console while Ehrich positioned himself back behind the equipment, clutching the lever to keep from being pulled away.

Ole Lukoje continued to climb along the floor, moving inch by inch toward Bess, who was now trying to move toward Ehrich.

Ba Tian reached out to catch hold of the console. Ehrich shot his foot out and stomped on the man's red hand. Ba Tian let go of the edge and the force of the void pulled him away.

"Noooooooo!!!" The crimson warlord screamed.

His body slammed into Ole Lukoje, knocking the raggedy man off balance. For a second, the one claw that was in the floor held, but the added weight of Ba Tian was too much and the claw slid out of the rock floor. The two men hurtled backward into the vortex. Their bodies were rent to pieces, each bit flying into the myriad of worlds that were flashing through the opening.

The crimson warlord and the raggedy man were gone forever.

"Ehrich!" Bess screamed. "I can't hang on any longer."

She clung to the console with one hand. He reached out and grabbed her arm just as her other hand slipped off. His arms felt like they were being ripped out of their sockets. He held onto her and started to reel her in. The force of the void was strong. He redoubled his efforts to hang on to her.

He felt her grip slipping. He tried to reposition his hold on her, but she continued to inch away from him.

"Bess! Hang on."

"Ehrich!"

Her hand slipped off and her body flew to the distortion field. Ehrich lunged, not for her but for the lever that controlled Demon Gate. He yanked it to the off position.

Too late. Bess flew into the vortex, but her body didn't split apart. Instead, it floated into the distortion field that wrapped around her. She howled in pain as the dimensional portal closed in around her.

"Bess!" Ehrich screamed.

Then the portal and Bess blinked out of existence.

"No!"

She was gone.

Ba Tian and Ole Lukoje had been defeated, but Ehrich had paid the ultimate price for victory. He stared at the empty space, willing the girl he loved to come back. Only cold air and silence greeted him.

—◦⋏⋏⋏◦—

Amina and Dash entered the chamber. With them was Mr. Serenity. Ehrich stiffened.

"Kifo?"

Amina waved him off.

"It's all right, Ehrich. It's Mr. Serenity. He's back. Kifo is no more. The Infinity Coil is destroyed."

"What? How?"

"It's a long story," she said. "What happened?"

Ehrich looked down at the floor. "They're gone. It's over."

HOME

In the aftermath of the battle, the group surveyed the Demon Gate chamber. Amina, Mr. Serenity, and Tesla had planned to go back to the surface to help Charlie and the hunters take down the rest of Farrier's soldiers. Tesla had access to the arsenal and the bomb that he had constructed. He was certain it would give them a distinct advantage in the fight.

They prepared to go but Ehrich and Dash remained.

"What are you doing?" Amina asked.

Ehrich said, "I made a promise that I mean to keep." He looked at Dash.

"We're going home?" his brother asked.

He nodded.

Tesla walked over and put his hand on Ehrich's shoulder. "You know you are welcome to stay in this world."

Mr. Serenity added. "We could use the two of you in the fight."

Ehrich shook his head. "There's nothing to keep me here

anymore. Tell Charlie I will miss him."

Tesla nodded.

Amina came over to them. "Ehrich, I am sorry for what you have lost, but know that you have saved worlds. Bess's sacrifice will be remembered."

He had no words. She kissed him on the cheek. "I know your heart belongs to Bess, but I will forever be your friend. If you ever need me, I will come to your call."

"Thanks, Amina, but I hope never to see anything but my world from this point on."

"I understand."

They parted. Ehrich took Dash's hand and walked to the alcove. "Mr. Tesla, can you find my world?"

"Let me see if I can." Tesla operated the controls on the console and Demon Gate opened up once again.

Ahead of them, the images of worlds cycled through. Dash squeezed Ehrich's hand when the Appleton graveyard appeared.

"Stop!" Dash squealed. "That's home. Right there."

Ehrich turned to Tesla. "I won't forget you. Thank you."

The trio waved back at him. Ehrich and Dash walked through and fell into the other side.

—◆◇◆—

Landing among the gravestones, Ehrich felt lighter than he had in years. The return home felt good. The air smelled familiar. Beside him, Dash acted like his old self again. Though they were both older now, they felt like they were kids again. They headed out of the graveyard and made their way to their home.

"You think mother and father are still in the same place?"

"Knowing them, they'd never leave."

"How do we explain where we were?"

"They always suspected I wanted to be in the circus. Maybe we can tell them we ran away to be entertainers."

Dash smiled. "Mother's going to be fit to be tied. Dad's going to yell at us for days."

"Yes, I can't wait."

"Me, too."

They sprinted to the apartment complex that was their home. When Ehrich reached the door, he opened it. Inside, his mother and father were seated at the table. Their eyes widened with surprise and wonder and recognition. "Ehrich! Dash!" They rushed over and hugged their sons, finally returned home.

—⁄⁄⁄—

Three years later, Ehrich cut a dashing figure in his black suit. He performed on stage as the great Harry Houdini. His assistant, Dash, had also filled out. The two of them performed Metamorphosis for an enthralled audience. Ehrich missed having the codex to project the image, and Dash hated to have to squeeze into the box to disappear, but they were making a name for themselves.

On this night, however, Dash was late with his entrance and the trick was ruined. The audience jeered the act and Ehrich had to leave the stage in shame. As soon as they were backstage, he tore a strip off his brother.

"Move faster. You can't dally on this."

"We need a bigger trunk. I can't fit in there anymore," Dash countered.

"No, you need to move faster or lose some weight."

"I'm telling you we need to build a bigger trunk."

"We can't afford to do that."

"Then scrap Metamorphosis out of the act and we'll come up with something else."

"No. It stays," Ehrich said. He clung to this act as the only thing that made him feel at home. Though he knew this was his dimension, he felt empty in this place.

"Well, either it goes or I do," Dash said.

"That can be arranged."

"You wouldn't dare. You can barely afford to pay me. Who's going to work for you for free?"

"Anyone is better than you, Dash!"

A cough interrupted their argument. Ehrich turned. From the wings, a beautiful young woman stepped forward. "I might have a solution."

It was Bess. Ehrich was at a loss for words. She was a little older and much thinner, but the face he knew so well was staring back at him. Was this a mirage or had she somehow miraculously found her way to him again?

"Hello. I'm sorry for eavesdropping, but you need a smaller assistant for that illusion."

Dash cocked his head to the side. "It's her. Isn't it?"

She smiled. "I see you kept your old magician's name. Harry Houdini. I like it."

"Bess? Is it you?"

She beamed. "In the flesh. More or less."

"What happened? How did you? I thought you were ..."

"I'm not quite sure what exactly happened. I landed in another dimension. Had to find my way to a portal. You can't imagine how hard it is to find one of those things. Took me forever. I wasn't going to leave you without an assistant."

"Don't you want to stay in your home world?" Ehrich asked. "I mean I don't want you to go, but this isn't your world."

"Anywhere that you are is my world."

He straightened up.

"Really?"

"Without a doubt."

He wrapped his arms around her. She returned the warm embrace. A rush of emotions filled his mind and heart, and all he wanted to do was kiss her.

He began to lean in, but Dash interrupted. "Um, does that mean she's in the act now?"

Ehrich glared at his brother.

"I'm just saying she's the right size for the trunk. You can do Metamorphosis with her, but where does that leave me?"

Ehrich growled. "Anywhere but here, Dash."

"Oh. Right." He backed out of the wings, leaving the two alone.

"Where were we?" Ehrich asked.

"I think right about here." She took his head in her hands and kissed him.

Now he felt like he was truly home.

THE END

Marty Chan